ZONE ELEVEN

& OTHER DOPE TALES

TIARA JANTÉ

Contents

To my Ancestors, who have empowered me in ways beyond expression. To my children, who are my every reason. To my mother, grandmother, auntie, siblings, niece, and nephews, who inspire me everyday. To my descendants who have carved my path. To my TF ∞.

ZONE ELEVEN: PART I

INCOMING

R egina woke, biked, showered, dressed. Smoothie blended, poured, keys grabbed, door locked. All by 7:30 am. Then, the drive: 40 minutes from home to Midtown Atlanta. She parked, exchanged smiles with the ever flirtatious security guard, then descended thirty stories into the heart of the Agency of Interstellar Affairs—AIA, headquarters. All routine, until it wasn't.

The morning at HQ unfolded in its familiar rhythm. Regina entered her office, deposited her belongings, skimmed through her day's agenda, and made the customary pilgrimage to the break room for her coffee fix. With a steaming mug in hand, she navigated the day's sequence of meetings, phone calls, a quick lunch, and the steady flow of emails, all punctuated by light-hearted exchanges with her colleagues. It was an ordinary day, adhering perfectly to the script of her daily routine. That is, until an abrupt deviation occurred. A subtle vibration from her cell phone as she prepared to leave for the weekend heralded a shift, a simple notification on the screen breaking the monotony:

"34.9490° N, 84.5805° W. Come alone."

Now, as Regina made her way along the dimly lit expanse, she couldn't help but berate herself for stepping out of her usual pattern—surrendering to such an impromptu impulse. This rash decision, she reflected, was sure to become a point of conversation with her therapist. The all-too-frequent reports of Black women disappearing without a trace was not lost on her. And yet, here she was, driving down the isolated backroads of Northern Georgia, moving towards coordinates that seemingly pointed straight to nowhere.

There was no room for doubt—she had double-checked the coordinates on her phone's map app and then cross-referenced them with the advanced tech at her office. Indeed, she was en route to an absolute void. Well, a void nestled within the vast forestry of Georgia's Cohutta Wilderness, to be precise. And although Regina was no stranger to the joys of camping, she much preferred the idea of spending a tranquil weekend curled up on her sofa, indulging in comfort food and binge-watching her favorite shows.

"So much for my weekend routine," Regina muttered, her gaze shifting back and forth between the road ahead and her car's navigation display.

But if she really thought about it—was anything in her life routine? As she drove, Regina's mind wandered to her recent promotion, a reminder of the unconventional path her life had always taken. Her thoughts drifted back to her college days, specifically her senior year, marking the start of her extraordinary journey. It was then when she was unexpectedly recruited into the research component of a secretive military group. The exact reason remained somewhat of a mystery to her. She only knew it had something to do with her exceptional scores on a test she barely recalled taking—a test that suggested she possessed capabilities she hadn't fully tapped into yet. But she embraced the opportunity—because why wouldn't she? This enigmatic beginning paved her way through the ranks, ultimately leading her to the AIA. Now, seven years into her career, she held the title of Director, a role as bewildering as the message that was now guiding her into the depths of the night.

The promotion was not without its challenges, having navigated spaces rarely graced by those who looked like her. Yet, beyond the accolades and the inevitable sacrifices, there was a singular, unexplainable encounter from her past that fueled her drive. That deep-seated curiosity about what exists beyond the stars, sparked by an experience too strange and too real, was the same force that compelled her towards the unknown coordinates tonight, despite every Black ass urge screaming for her to stick with her routine and stay the course that was her life. Then again, some would argue this was pretty par for the course.

Arriving at her destination, Regina shifted her car into PARK, and exited the car. But as she stepped out into the vast, silent emptiness, doubt crept in. She scanned her surroundings. Just as the map suggested—nothing—just a single, empty road beneath a thick canopy of trees that offered no clues, no structures, nothing to justify her presence there. An emptiness so glaring she couldn't help but consider whether she'd been pranked, or even worse, set up somehow. "What the hell is this?" she murmured, her nerves getting the best of her.

Just then, her cell phone vibrated, a new message lighting up the screen:

"I'm right ahead of you. Walk forward five steps, and you'll see."

Already on guard, Regina glanced around once more, nervously. Was she being watched? Yet, despite the strangeness of the request, she complied, because at this point, the entire situation was strange. After shutting off her engine, and closing her car door, she began to walk forward from her car. "One... two... three... four...five," she counted, her voice unsteady against the silence.

With the fifth step, the ground transformed, a structure sprouting from the earth itself. There, a door awaited her, plain yet unmistakably out of place in the desolate landscape.

Consciously ignoring the "Don't go in there, girl," echoing within her head, she stepped through the door and immediately began descending, the ground beneath her now an elevator pulling her into the unknown.

Regina's descent was swift, the shift from movement to stillness catching her off guard. The door before her opened smoothly, and after catching her breath, she found herself stepping into what could only be described as the nexus of cutting-edge technology. Around her was an expanse that seemed to defy the limits of all that she knew; holographic displays hovering over workstations, projecting digital streams into the air, while the background hum of machinery pulsed with life; innovations far removed from her reality.

Absorbing her new environment, a voice, both clear and soothing, permeated the space. "Welcome, Dr. Reyes. I am S.O.P.H.I.A., Source of Origins, Preserver of Heritage, Intelligence, and Autonomy. I hail from a dimension known as the Node."

In response, a sweeping hologram flickered around Regina, enveloping her in the breathtaking vistas of a world that wasn't her own. "This," S.O.P.H.I.A. continued, "is the Node, conceived as a sanctuary from human adversity, where magic and technology blend to create harmony."

But, Regina wasn't merely observing the Node; she was part of it, enveloped in its essence. Such an immersive experience was thought to be the realm of advanced, almost mythical alien technology, whispered about in the corridors of the AIA for its ability to craft indistinguishably real alternate dimensions. Yet, here she was, suddenly thrust into such a reality, a gift—or perhaps a revelation—courtesy of S.O.P.H.I.A. This unexpected transition sparked a question that sent ripples through her mind: what was S.O.P.H.I.A.?

At that moment, a pivotal memory surged into Regina's thoughts, catapulting her back to the cusp of adulthood. At 17, she was tangled in the typical quandaries of youth—who she should take to prom, which HBCU she should attend. It was during this period of innocuous indecision that the extraordinary breached her life.

One evening, as she sat on her back porch, enveloped in the quiet of the night, Regina was suddenly and inexplicably torn from her familiar reality. She found herself plunged into an indescribable ordeal, far removed from anything she could understand. Then, just as suddenly as it had happened, she was returned to her porch, with no memory of where she had been or what had transpired. Yet, an unshakeable certainty lingered within her—a profound awareness that she had indeed been taken somewhere, and something *had* happened there.

This unmistakable encounter with the unknown carved a deep mark within Regina's sense of self, serving as an invisible compass that directed her decisions and career path thereafter. An experience so profound yet so personal, she never shared it with a soul. Now, amidst the wonders of the Node—a domain where the extraordinary was just another part of the everyday—Regina saw the fabric of her past experiences woven seamlessly with the present, resonating with the silent story of her abduction, a chapter of her life she had tried to ignore.

Regina's thoughts were snatched back into the present as she found herself standing in the middle of the Node. Her eyes widened, taking in the sights around her. Buildings, if you could still call them that, intertwined with the natural world around them, draped in greenery, with solar panels stretching upwards like modern obelisks seeking the sun's blessing. Water flowed in purposeful paths around her, a network of life that connected everything.

She marveled at how technology and nature didn't just coexist here—they were interwoven, indistinguishable from one another, a testament to a society that had mastered true harmony. It was a stark contrast to the world she knew, where such balance remained a distant goal.

"The Node is the epitome of creativity, a place where technology enhances tradition, creating a society that values both progress and heritage," S.O.P.H.I.A. began, her voice painting a picture of serene existence far removed from Earth's chaos. But then, the tone changed, introducing a shadow to the utopia. "Yet, even in paradise, there are trials. The Node now faces a threat like no other, a force that strikes without warning, consuming all in its path. This menace is known as Zone E leven."

The imagery around Regina morphed to depict Zone Eleven not merely as a place but as an insatiable force, one that threatened to dissolve the very essence of reality itself, putting both Earth and the Node's very existence in jeopardy.

"It operates beyond the realms of kindness or cruelty," S.O.P.H.I.A. elucidated. "It embodies a living, ambivalent force, indifferent to the fates it intertwines with. Through my transition from a human entity to... something else, I've gained an unparalleled understanding of its essence. This force, it's part of an ancient cycle—one of death, creation, and rebirth, an all-consuming energy that sustains itself by drawing in everything around it. It's not just about destruction; it's about transformation and the perpetual motion of existence. I can perceive its approach, sense the subtle shifts it incites in the fabric of reality. It's drawing nearer, its presence signifying a time of change and renewal, albeit in ways that might challenge our comprehension, and diminish us in the process."

"Wait, you referred to yourself as something else? What exactly do you mean by that, S.O.P.H.I.A.? What exactly are you?" Regina interrupted.

S.O.P.H.I.A. paused briefly before answering. "I exist beyond human constraints of perception and being. There is no simple term for what I've become. But concerning Zone Eleven, it's not an object or place—it's conscious, alive in ways I'm still grasping. Its nature defies our moral compass, existing outside our universe's norms. My transformation grants me glimpses into its consciousness, insights we might leverage."

Regina's mind whirled. "Okay, but what can we do? How do we shield our worlds from this Zone Eleven?"

"A viable path lies in a cloaked planet, just half a light year away. It must be incorporated into our contingency strategy. As the data stands currently, the onset of Zone Eleven is unavoidable, and this planet represents our only refuge."

Bewildered, Regina countered, "Hold on... how do you expect me to lead such a mission? What resources do we have? What is our timeframe for all this?"

"You were selected for your extraordinary insight, Dr. Reyes. We have resources ready, here and elsewhere, to support this mission. But, our time frame is tight—less than five years before Zone Eleven's impact is irrevocable."

"Five years? With half a year travel time? That hardly gives us time to prepare. Who's part of the crew? How do we approach a planet that's hidden?"

"The mission you'll lead requires a diverse team, Dr. Reyes. Beyond the scientists, engineers, and strategists, you will need individuals skilled in the arcane arts..."

"So, you mean people like rootworkers and psychics and what not?" Regina sighed. "Chiile... I know you..."

"Correct," S.O.P.H.I.A. interrupted. "And no, I am not... lying. Dr. Reyes, this mission is unique— it transcends scientific exploration, requiring an amalgamation of knowledge, both empirical and mystical. The veiling of this planet suggests a metaphysical defense mechanism or perhaps a sentient choice. To unveil its secrets and ensure our survival, your team must be as diverse in skills as the mysteries you seek to unravel."

"And how are we to find these... unconventional experts?"

"I've identified two key individuals for the mission," S.O.P.H.I.A. declared. "First is Aja Jones, a 28-year-old rootworker, well-engaged online and close to your Atlanta headquarters. Then there's Khalil Brown, a 30-year-old psychic medium who owns a metaphysical shop in Philadelphia. Locate them, gain their cooperation, and I will contact you again."

As the conversation concluded, the laboratory began to shift, gently returning Regina to the surface world, her mind teeming with thoughts of the Node, S.O.P.H.I.A.'s intel, and the looming threat of Zone Eleven.

Back in her car, the engine still running, the stillness of the night around her felt more pronounced. She started the car, then turned on some music, letting it fill the space in a feeble attempt to quell her racing thoughts. But her brief respite was cut short by her phone ringing—a call from Sean, her brother, who typically communicated in texts and memes rather than calls. His name flashing on the display sent a jolt of apprehension through her. With a deep breath, she answered, the static of the connection signaling the start of another unexpected chapter of her night.

"Regina, sis, are you there?" There was a note of urgency and panic in his voice.

"Yes, Sean, I'm here. What's up?"

"It's... well, shit... I don't even know how to put this," Sean's voice faltered, a notable hesitance punctuating his words. "Listen... I just watched the woman I've been seeing get absorbed into a—" his voice cut abruptly.

"Absorbed into what? Sean? Are you there?" Regina pressed, her concern escalating as she clenched the steering wheel tighter. But no further explanation came, only the silence of a dead line. She pulled over, inhaling deep breaths to calm her already torrent nerves. Home was several hours away, Sean seemed to be in trouble, and her nerves were on edge. She needed to stop, to think.

"Hotel," she typed into her navigation, desperate for a pause from the night's madness. A nearby roadside motel popped up, a short-term escape. She headed there, knowing full well that rest was a hopeful thought, the abrupt end to her call with Sean weighing heavily on her.

An hour later, in the modest motel room, Regina's fingers hovered over her laptop's keyboard, her room illuminated only by a lamp on a nightstand and the soft glow of her laptop screen. A pizza box lay open beside her, barely-eaten, a testament to her distracted appetite. She'd tried Sean's number several times, but was met with the familiar, impersonal tone of his voicemail. "Sean, it's me again," she sighed into the phone. "I really need to talk to you. Call me back as soon as you get this, okay? I'm worried." She ended the call, feeling the weight of concern for her brother pressing down on her.

Turning back to her laptop, Regina's brow furrowed as she typed in search terms, hoping to unearth anything on S.O.P.H.I.A. or Zone Eleven in AIA's database. But each query returned more questions than answers, the digital paper trail as elusive as mist. *What are you hiding?* she thought, her frustration growing.

As Regina sat in the dim glow of her laptop screen, a whisper of thought brushed against her consciousness—a lingering echo of S.O.P.H.I.A.'s description of Zone Eleven. "Death, creation, rebirth…" she murmured to herself, a realization dawning. These weren't just concepts; they were keys.

"Okay, let's see where you lead," she spoke to the silence of the room, her fingers poised above the keyboard. Hesitantly, then with growing purpose, she typed the words "Death, creation, and rebirth" into the search bar.

"This has to mean something," Regina whispered under her breath.

As Regina's search results unfurled on the screen, her attention snagged on a result detailing the Kongo Cosmogram, or *Dikenga Dia Kongo*. The room around her stilled.

"This… this is it," she murmured, tracing the lines of text with a finger as if to physically connect with the information. "The Kongo cosmogram… it's not just a symbol, it's a depiction of the cycle of existence, bridging the physical world, *Ku Nseke*, with the spiritual realm, *Ku Mpémba*, through the *Kalûnga* line—a river that navigates between the two realms, embodying the journey of life."

She paused, absorbing the historical depth of the cosmogram. "So, before European contact in 1482, the BaKongo culture had this… this cosmic map that laid out their identity within the universe. It survived, making its way to the Americas, engraved in pottery, and drawn on church walls by enslaved BaKongo people."

Regina leaned back, her mind racing. *"Kalûnga... the spark of creation that became a great force, birthing the universe. It's the threshold between worlds, guiding the BaKongo through life's stages."* She chuckled lightly, despite the gravity of her research. "Here I am, trying to make sense of Zone Eleven, and our ancestors had it figured out centuries ago."

"Now... if the Cosmogram represents the sun's journey—conception, birth, maturity, death, then everything cycles through these stages... Earth, ideas, societies... even cosmic phenomena like Zone Eleven." Regina tapped her fingers on the night stand beside her, piecing together the connections. "S.O.P.H.I.A. mentioned a cycle, and here it is, laid out in the Kongo cosmogram."

She stood up, stretching, her gaze fixed on the night sky visible from her window. "The Yowa cross, it's not just about direction; it's about transformation, the endless loop of becoming and unbecoming. If Zone Eleven is part of this cycle... then understanding it, maybe even navigating it, could be within our reach."

With renewed vigor, Regina sat down to document her findings. "Tomorrow, I'll need to explain how an ancient African symbol might hold the key to saving us from a cosmic event. No pressure, indeed." She laughed softly, the sound a mix of excitement and the weight of responsibility. "But first, I have a meeting with Finch and Marino. I'll need their minds, skepticism and all, to unravel this further."

Determined, Regina powered down her laptop, her thoughts already on the discussions to come, the strategies to devise, and the incredible task ahead of her.

The next morning, as sunlight crept across the room, the previous night's revelations sprung to life in her mind. She reached for her secure device, then typed out a message with deliberate care:

"Sorry for the Saturday morning text, but urgent meeting needed at HQ. Something significant has come up."

Then, with a deep breath, she sent the message off to Agents Finch and Marino, hoping it conveyed the appropriate amount of urgency.

Next, she freshened up, checked out at the front desk, then headed to her car. The drive to AIA HQ was a blur of anticipation and rehearsed explanations. "How do I explain this without sounding like a lunatic?" she thought, navigating the road to Midtown on autopilot. "And I'm definitely not bringing up... *that* night."

Upon arrival, she found Finch and Marino awaiting her, their expressions a mix of curiosity and weariness.

"Reyes, early Saturday mornings better come with good reasons," Finch greeted, his annoyance evident in his tone.

Marino offered a lighter touch, his smile easy and welcoming. "What's got you stirring up the pot so early, Reyes?"

She allowed herself a small smile in return, "Let's just say I stumbled upon somethin g... quite unexpected. Inside, I'll explain."

Gathering in the briefing room, Regina leaned back in a chair slightly, sensing the gravity of the room but also recognizing the need to ease into the revelation with a bit of levity. "So, last night, as I was getting ready to leave for the day, preparing for an exciting weekend on my big, comfy couch, BOOM!, I get coordinates pinged to my phone. Not spam, not a wrong number, but a direct invite to the twilight zone," she began, a wry smile playing on her lips as she glanced at Finch and Marino's intrigued faces.

"Next thing I know, I'm driving to the middle of nowhere, thinking either this is the best kept secret of our time, or I've finally cracked," she continued, her humor underlining the surreal nature of her experience. "And there I was, expecting maybe a secret facility, a hidden bunker, or at the very least, a welcome party."

Marino chuckled, "Let me guess, you found a spaceship instead?"

"Almost as good," Regina replied, rolling her eyes playfully. "I step out, and the ground opens up, swallowing me up... into this... let's call it an 'underground tech wonderland.' And that's where I meet S.O.P.H.I.A., our guide to the cosmos, or so it claims."

Finch, ever the skeptic, interjected, "And you just went with it?"

Regina nodded, "I did." Then, she leaned in with a twinkle of both seriousness and mischief in her eyes. "So, I'm inside this rabbit hole, and S.O.P.H.I.A. throws me this curveball called Zone Eleven. And it's big— I mean REAL big— like Extinction Level Event big. According to S.O.P.H.I.A., Zone Eleven is not just some cosmic bully lurking in the shadows; it's more like the universe's way of hitting the reset button. Creation, death, rebirth—lather, rinse, repeat. And it's got this energy, something out of a sci-fi flick, that's tied up in the same loop reflected in the wisdom of old school African Cosmology."

Regina's tone took on a conspiratorial edge, "But here's where it gets spicy. This cycle, while fascinating in a 'circle of life' kind of way, is barreling towards us and the Node like a cosmic freight train. And by the way, the Node is not just any stop along the way. Imagine if Silicon Valley and Hogwarts had a baby, and that baby decided to set up shop in a dimension with better décor. It's a marvel—tech and magic living in harmony, creating a place where the impossible seems pretty much Tuesday— and I was in there."

She leaned back, a satisfied grin on her face at their rapt attention. "So, yes, while Zone Eleven is busy doing its cosmic two-step of destruction and rebirth, it's eyeballing both Earth and the Node like we're the next big thing in intergalactic real estate. S.O.P.H.I.A.'s game plan? Dive deep into this cycle, figure it out, round up a rootworker and a psychic she's handpicked, then locate and terraform a hidden planet as our only means of saving humanity and the Node— in five years' time. No pressure, right?"

The revelation hung in the air, a mix of disbelief and concern on Finch and Marino's faces.

"Five years to save the world, huh? And I thought my schedule was packed," Marino quipped, the tension in the room easing slightly.

Regina smiled, appreciating Marino's attempt to lighten the mood. "But seriously," she continued, the smile fading, "this is our reality now. S.O.P.H.I.A. has given us a roadmap, but it's on us to follow it, to understand this cycle and find a way to that planet."

Finch adjusted his posture, leaning in with a blend of curiosity and caution sharpening his features. "Hold on a second, Reyes," he interjected, his skepticism not entirely swept away. "Before we chart a course through uncharted cosmos based on this S.O.P.H.I.A.'s intel, can we just pause and assess? Exactly who, or what, is S.O.P.H.I.A., and how do we know we're putting our chips on the right square? I mean, entrusting the fate of Earth to an entity we don't even understand—like, how do we verify its credibility?"

But, before Regina could formulate a response, the familiar chime of an incoming alert interrupted their briefing. Each agent's phone lit up simultaneously, an uncommon occurrence that signaled the urgency of the matter at hand. The message was clear: a virtual meeting was scheduled immediately concerning an interstellar anomaly—a directive that brooked no delay.

Without missing a beat, Marino sprang into action, pulling up the virtual meeting interface on the large screen that dominated one wall of the briefing room. "Looks like it's about to get spicier," he said as the digital conference room came into focus.

As the faces of various international colleagues populated the screen, a sense of global camaraderie against an unknown threat underscored the meeting. Leading the conference was Agent Kiana Tate, their colleague stationed at the International Space Station 2.0— the new and improved lunar headquarters. Kiana worked in a top secret department of the

AIA— the Anomalous Events Sector. Her image, framed against the backdrop of Earth seen from space, lent her words an added weight.

"Good morning, everyone," Kiana began, her tone serious yet composed. "We've convened this emergency briefing today because we've detected a massive, enigmatic energy signature an unknown amount of light years away, moving with a purpose and direction that suggest it's no natural cosmic event. Its trajectory? Heading straight for Earth."

The room fell silent as the magnitude of Kiana's announcement settled in. "This event is unprecedented and we've just received some additional intel from a unique source—who I understand that you, Dr. Reyes, may already be in contact with."

"Yes, are you referring to S.O.P.H.I.A.?" Regina replied.

As Kiana detailed her findings, Regina muted her mic, then turned to Finch and Marino, "Welp.. this seems like the confirmation we needed. S.O.P.H.I.A. warned us about Zone Eleven, and now we're seeing additional evidence of its existence and threat. We need to act, and fast."

The revelation from Kiana, paired with S.O.P.H.I.A.'s intel, galvanized the team. Despite the unknowns surrounding S.O.P.H.I.A., the immediate danger presented by the cosmic anomaly offered no room for doubt or delay. The path forward was clear: understand the cycle, trust in the guidance they'd received, and mobilize to protect Earth and the Node from the cosmic threat on their doorstep. But first... they needed to find Aja Jones and Khalil Brown.

To be continued in Part II...

THREADBARE

As the first rays of dawn flickered through her window blinds, Karyn let out a heavy sigh. Reluctantly, she pushed herself upright and slid slowly to the edge of the bed. She shuddered as her feet met the hardwood floor, the morning chill greeting her feet sharply. But the ritual that loomed before her chilled her even more, its hunger for the vitality in her veins palpable even in these quiet moments.

The house's silence was as thick as fog, a living thing that whispered of lost freedoms and a fate no longer her own. College had offered a brief respite, a fleeting glimpse of a life unshackled, until Elaine's illness yanked her back, tethering her to a curse she now bore in isolation.

Her grandmother, Elaine, had been the unwavering guardian of her family's twisted legacy until her death. But nowadays, the idea of 'legacy' seemed subjective, because Karyn often wondered whether Elaine's death was just the final, cruel handoff of a curse dressed as a family heirloom.

For a while after Elaine's death, things seemed normal. Karyn even managed to fall in love, marry, and have a daughter of her own. But no amount of love could shield Karyn from her internal decay— a side effect of the monthly bloodletting ritual she was forced to take part in since her youth. Shortly after their daughter Sia was born, her ex-husband Kyle left, the first casualty of the curse's cruel demands. Gradually, her friends pulled away too, unable to penetrate the barrier of secrecy and sorrow enveloping her. But it was the distance from her daughter, Sia, that cut the deepest. Sia, the single joy in her otherwise bleak existence, had become yet another sacrifice to the altar of her ancestral obligation.

Sending Sia away to live with her father felt like a knife through the heart. But Karyn knew it was a necessary cruelty to try and spare her from the dark fate awaiting every firstborn daughter in their line. And while deep down she sensed she couldn't shield her daughter forever— she would do everything in her power to try.

As Karyn moved through her morning routine, each action was layered with a heaviness that made the air around her thick. She stood under the shower, letting the hot water cascade over her body, attempting to cleanse not just her skin but the dread that clung to her. Brushing her teeth was another step in the charade of normalcy, the mint of the toothpaste a welcome contrast to the bitterness that filled her mouth at the thought of what was to come. Dressing was a deliberate affair; she chose her clothes with a mind toward what was practical for the day's grim tasks, her movements slow, laden with silent protest. She avoided her own gaze in the mirror, unwilling to confront the resignation in her eyes.

Sending a good morning text to Sia was a brief moment of lightness in her heavy morning. "Have a great day, baby girl. Thinking of you," she typed, a small smile forming on her lips. It was a momentary escape, a fleeting reminder of love in the midst of her encroaching obligations.

Next, she checked her email, scanning for messages about new projects and brand partnerships. As an influential designer, her social feeds were a testament to her creativity and a lifeline to the outside world. Turning to her emails, Karyn donned her professional mask, engaging with inquiries and opportunities that spoke of a life beyond the curse. *If only they knew*, she thought, as she replied with practiced ease. Her social media updates were a masterclass in illusion, each post a carefully constructed lie. "Smile for the camera, hide the chains," she mused, her heart heavy.

Fixing coffee and a quick breakfast was the last act of her morning's performance. The aroma of the coffee filled the kitchen, a comforting ritual in its own right, but today it was just another step toward the inevitable. Reluctantly, she took small bites of toast, not out of hunger, but with the recognition that she needed to sustain her strength for the day ahead.

Finally, Karyn made her way to the sewing room, the host to her familial curse. Each step felt like moving against a current, her body a vessel for a thousand reluctant movements. And there it was, The Celestial Quilt, hanging ominously at its regular spot on the wall. The story of the Quilt was a heavy one, woven with acts of sacrifice and something... else. Her ancestor, Alice, a talented seamstress, but an even more talented conjure woman, had sought to protect her family from the gnawing jaws of destitution. In her desperation, she reached out to a spirit unfamiliar, one not of their ancestral lineage but powerful in its own right. Under the glow of a blood-red moon, a pact was made, sealed with the creation of The Celestial Quilt.

The Quilt was nothing short of a cosmic marvel, its squares adorned with celestial symbols and perfectly etched geometric patterns that transcended the fabric, woven with threads that seemed to stretch across galaxies. But its centerpiece, a circle of arrows spiraled counter-clockwise around a cross, was the true focal point. "This symbol," Elaine had said, "is our homage to our roots, a sacred emblem of our homeland. Brought to this land in the hearts of our enslaved ancestors, it's a testament to resilience, to our enduring spirit." Karyn had watched as Elaine's fingers traced the circle of arrows with reverence. "In this pattern, our lineage converges with the cosmos, binding us to the past and guiding us forward. This is not just heritage; it's a reminder of our connection to the universe, through the cycle of creation, death, and rebirth."

But the Quilt, for all its beauty and the provisions it offered, came with a price. It required sustenance, a bond renewed with the blood of Alice's lineage. And over the years, the family had complied, renewing their pact every 28 days without cease. In exchange for their sacrifice, the family's needs were met exceedingly—as long as it was given respect, obedience, and most importantly—blood.

Karyn thought back to her first ritual, on the day she turned 16. In the quiet of their sewing room, Karyn and her grandmother Elaine, adorned in white dresses and head wraps, stood before The Quilt as it billowed gently, almost breathing in anticipation. Elaine turned to Karyn, "Today, you join a lineage of strength, Karyn. This is not just a tradition; it's our covenant with the past and future," she said, her words devoid of warmth, imbued instead with grave significance.

Karyn's heart raced, her stomach knotting. She had always known this day would come, yet facing it filled her with a mix of fear and a desperate desire not to disappoint Elaine. "Grandma... I'm scared. I don't think I'm ready for this," Karyn whispered, her voice trembling.

Elaine cupped Karyn's face in her hands. "Fear is part of our heritage, child. Our strength don't lie in fearlessness. It lies in confronting our fear, accepting it, and fulfilling our duties." Elaine's gaze locked onto Karyn's, "None of us were ready for this burden— but choice ain't a luxury we have. You understand?"

Taking a deep, steadying breath, Karyn managed a nod. Elaine then opened a drawer in the altar situated beneath the Quilt, retrieving a small, worn pouch. From it, she produced two silver sewing needles. "With these, we tether ourselves to the Quilt, ensuring our protection and prosperity through sacrifice. Your blood will merge with its threads, weaving you into the fabric of our legacy."

Karyn's hands shook as she took the needle. The cold metal felt like ice against her fingertips. Together, they pricked their fingers, ruby droplets welling at the surface. Karyn watched, mesmerized and horrified, as Elaine guided her finger against the Quilt. The cloth awakened then, its threads writhing slightly as they absorbed the blood.

"It feeds, Karyn, but it also gives. Our family has thrived under its care," Elaine whispered, her eyes fixed on the Quilt. "Your blood is now woven into its legacy."

As the Quilt fed, Karyn felt a pull, a slight tingling at her finger that morphed into a wave of heat that coursed through her veins. The sensation was overwhelming, leaving Karyn feeling drained, a husk left behind by the Quilt's insatiable hunger. It was an intimate violation, a vampire siphoning life, leaving her exposed and vulnerable. In the aftermath, as the last of the warmth ebbed away, Karyn realized the full extent of what the ritual meant.

It wasn't just about protection and prosperity; it was a pact that demanded perpetual sacrifices, a bond that took far more than it gave. She was part of the Quilt now, her blood mingled with those who had come before her, but at what cost? The so-called legacy Elaine spoke of with reverence was really a curse, a silent overseer that watched, waited, and fed upon each generation of her family.

Glancing away from the Quilt, Karyn powered on her sewing machine, and began her day's work. As her hands maneuvered the fabric and thread, her mind wandered, not to the task at hand, but through the cold memories of her upbringing. The house, with its looming shadows and silent spaces, had never offered warmth or comfort. Instead, it was a constant reminder of her isolation, a mausoleum for the living, presided over by her grandmother Elaine.

Karyn's thoughts drifted to her parents, their smiles frozen in time, their lives cut tragically short in a car wreck when she was ten. The accident had not just taken them; it had unceremoniously thrust her into the care of Elaine, her father's mother, a woman as stern and impenetrable as the house itself. It seemed almost like a cruel twist of destiny that brought her to Elaine's doorstep, for Elaine had only one child—Karyn's dad, who had escaped the family's curse by virtue of his gender.

Growing up, Karyn quickly learned that the curse that had bypassed her father was waiting for her, a silent predator biding its time. Elaine saw to it that early on Karyn was made aware of the responsibilities that awaited her, and hinted at the wrath that could follow if she refused. The house, with its oppressive atmosphere and the ever-present

Quilt, made sure she was aware as well—a destiny that was sealed the moment her parents' car veered off the road.

In the stillness of that room, as Karyn's thoughts danced between duty and destiny, a whisper cut through the hum of the sewing machine, chilling despite its softness. "Feed me," it hissed, a voice as familiar as it was unwelcome.

Karyn froze. She knew that voice, knew what it demanded, and she hated it. She hated the way the Quilt hungered, its whispers growing more insistent with each ritual. And she hated even more the idea of Sia, her bright, vibrant daughter, being pulled into this ancient, somber duty. It was one of the silent reliefs in the wake of her divorce from Kyle—Sia spending most of her days away from this house at her father's, away from the Quilt's sinister gaze. But lately, the whispers had grown louder, more demanding. With Sia approaching 16, the Quilt seemed eager for an introduction, and Karyn knew she couldn't hide Sia forever.

The silence in the room deepened, as the Quilt waited for Karyn to oblige its request. But Karyn was wary. She had long accepted that the legacy of The Celestial Quilt, of her family's pact with something far beyond the ordinary, was now hers. And for a while Karyn performed her rituals without hesitation— settling into a silent acknowledgement and resolve. This resolve was tested, however, on a day that would carve itself into Karyn's memory, a moment that would redefine her relationship with her daughter.

It was a routine night, the house enveloped in quiet, the world outside oblivious to the ancient rites taking place within. Karyn was engrossed in the ritual, the needle pricking her finger, when Sia, curious and silent as a shadow, wandered in. The look of sheer terror on Sia's face as she witnessed the Quilt consuming her mother's blood, the threads pulsating with a life of their own, shattered Karyn's heart.

"Mommy, what's happening?" Sia's voice, filled with fear and confusion, pierced the solemn atmosphere. Yanking her hand away, Karyn rushed to her young daughter, scooping her into her arms, her own heart racing.

"It's okay baby, it's just... it's a special project," Karyn stumbled over her words, her mind racing to shield Sia from the truth. "A story for grown-ups. You're safe, I promise."

But the damage was done. Sia's eyes, wide and filled with unspoken questions, haunted Karyn long after she had soothed her back to sleep. That night, as Sia lay dreaming of innocent tales, Karyn made a vow. The fear in Sia's eyes was a mirror to her own childhood terrors, reflections of a legacy she never asked for. It was then she decided that Sia's exposure to this part of her life would end. From that day forward, Sia would live at her father's house, away from the secrets and shadows that clung to the fabric of their family's history. But the distance between her and her daughter was just as draining as the Quilt, and Karyn didn't know how much more she could take.

"This legacy... it's mine to bear, but it's also mine to redefine," she affirmed to the quiet room. The realization didn't lighten the burden, but it did sharpen her sense of agency. Elaine had lived her life in service to this legacy, and now Karyn stood at a crossroads, facing a decision as to whether she would as well.

Karyn respected her lineage and the strength of the women who came before her, but the literal truth of the Quilt's demands had always been a point of contention within her logical mind. Yet, there was no denying the reality of its hunger, the weight of its gaze upon her as she worked, as she lived. Now, faced with another whispered demand, Karyn chose rebellion.

"Not today," she finally whispered back. She didn't want to perform the ritual, to give in to the Quilt's demands. But the Quilt's request lingered, a subtle caress against her mind, a reminder of the pact that bound her family to this otherworldly entity.

As Karyn resumed her work, the room grew a bit darker, the corners filling up with shadows that seemed just a bit too eager to creep closer. A chill trickled down her spine, uninvited and unwelcome. "Probably just the AC," she mumbled to herself, though the back of her mind whispered doubts she wasn't keen to entertain.

The sudden buzz of her phone sliced through the thickening silence, a welcome distraction. Sia's grinning face popped up on the screen, a snapshot from a sunnier day, both in weather and in spirit. "Miss you, Mom," the text underneath read, simple words that tugged at Karyn's heartstrings with unexpected force. She tapped out a response, her fingers a little too quick, a little too eager to send love and promises of time she hoped to make. But the moment she tapped send, a strange unease settled over her, the air around her noticeably heavier.

Then, out of the corner of her eye, Karyn caught something—a flutter, a shift in the air. It yanked her from her thoughts, her eyes snapping to the Quilt. She watched as it rippled, a gentle wave passing over its surface. Her breath hitched, a cold finger trailing across her skin. "All in my head," she tried to convince herself, willing away the unease that thickened the air around her. Yet, the room continued to close in, shadows deepening into something more sinister.

"Feed me, Karyn." The Quilt's voice was more insistent now, a whisper that felt like a shout in the increasingly oppressive silence. Her heart kicked against her ribs, a frantic rhythm trying to break free from the fear that clenched it.

But Karyn stood her ground, even though every instinct screamed at her to flee. "No," she whispered back. "I won't."

The Quilt stirred again, this time more violently, agitated by her refusal. The air in the room shifted even more, growing frigid. Karyn could feel its gaze upon her, a physical weight that demanded submission. "Feed meeeeee.... NOWWWW!"

"I said NO!" Karyn's voice was stronger now, bolstered by the surge of rebellion that filled her. She wouldn't be swayed, wouldn't give in to Alice's pact. This legacy of sacrifice and spiritual bargains was one she no longer intended to uphold, especially if it meant ensnaring Sia in the same familial chains. Yet, the Quilt continued to pulse with a life of its own, its patterns swirling, shifting in ways that defied logic. It was the embodiment of history and power, of bargains made under blood-red moons, and it did not take kindly to being denied. And as the shadows in the room danced and coalesced into forms too ephemeral to understand, Karyn could sense the reality of what her defiance might bring.

It was apparent that battlelines had been drawn, but Karyn was undeterred. She would be the first to push back against the tide, the first to question the cost of their prosperity and the first to say, "Enough!"

And suddenly, all was still.

"...the fuck?" Karyn paused, wondering if the Quilt had actually listened to her. Was it over? Could she finally step away from this nightmare? She studied the Quilt, cautiously waiting for it to provide answers. A notification from her cell phone yanked her from her thoughts. As her gaze flitted to her cellphone's homescreen, 3:00 PM stared back, a reminder of the day's fleeting nature.

"Damn it, this dress ain't gonna to finish itself," she muttered under her breath. But as she attempted to resume her work, the sewing machine sputtered and died, plunging the room back into silence. Karyn's attention snapped to the Quilt once more, witnessing the patterns begin to animate more violently now.

"That's it! I'm done with this shit!" she yelled, her voice echoing off the walls. Rising from her chair, a heavy sigh escaped her lips. "Why can't this nightmare end?" she said as she exited the sewing room. The door clicked shut behind her, the sound reverberating the potential consequences of her defiance, its finality an echo of her ongoing struggle with the legacy she so desperately wished to leave behind.

Hunger clawed at Karyn, perhaps a side effect of her anxiety or the shadow of depression that loomed over her. Food, in these moments, served as a rare comfort. Opting for grilled chicken atop a fresh bed of greens, she directed her thoughts away from the Quilt. Her mind wandered to brighter corners: Sia's latest successes at school, which brought a sense of pride; thoughts of Sean, whose companionship occasionally pierced her solitude, and the elusive sound of her own laughter, a melody so distant she struggled to remember its last genuine appearance. Beyond the memories of college freedom and the transient happiness of her marriage to Kyle, joy seemed like a foreign concept, leaving her to wonder when life had shifted from living to merely existing.

After eating, Karyn stood in her steam-filled bathroom, facing her reflection. The mirror, foggy at the edges, framed her face in a way that highlighted the toll her life had taken on. "Shit... when did I become so damn skinny?" she whispered, tracing the lines etched by worry and sleepless nights. The water's warmth was a temporary balm, but her thoughts, ever restless, eventually returned to the Quilt.

Later, settling into the comforting embrace of her bed, Karyn dialed Sia's number, seeking the grounding presence of her daughter's voice. "Hey, honey, how was your day?"

"Hey, Mom! School was okay, but guess what? Ashley's having a boy! I'm gonna have a little brother!" Sia's excitement bubbled through the line.

"That's amazing, sweetheart! I'm so happy for you. You're going to be the best big sister," Karyn replied, her heart swelling with pride mixed with a pang of longing for the closeness of her daughter.

Their conversation ventured through Sia's school life, her friends, and the small details that painted a picture of her world—a world Karyn felt both connected to and distanced from. "I miss you, baby girl. Let's plan a day out, just you and me," Karyn suggested, a promise to bridge the gap between them.

"Miss you too, Mom. Can't wait!"

With the end of their call, the silence of the house wrapped around Karyn like a cold blanket. Glancing at the time, Karyn sighed as she took in the hour. It was only 8PM. She was nobody's grandma, yet here she was, already tucked into her bed. Then, as Karyn stared at her phone, a plan formulated in her mind. She typed out a message, each word dripping with an unspoken invitation, "Feeling a bit restless tonight... could use some company. Interested?"

Sean's response was quick, laced with the same energy, "Should I bring anything besides myself?"

A smile played on Karyn's lips as she typed back, "Just bring some stamina. It's been a long day and I need rounds."

Sean played along, "Aight then. Stamina packed and ready. Be there soon."

As Karyn set her phone down, a fleeting sense of excitement coursed through her. Finally, a break from the relentless pressure of the Quilt. But even with her excitement for the activities ahead, she knew her escape would be short lived— no matter how much stamina Sean brought along with him.

As Karyn guided Sean into her dimly lit bedroom, her anticipation was electric. This was not about romance; it was a tacit pact of longing and necessity. Their interactions always lacked warmth, devoid of the tender journey of discovering affection. What they shared was sheer, unbridled urgency.

Without hesitation, Karyn prompted Sean onto her bed, then stood before him, slowly undoing her robe, letting it pool at her feet. She paused, allowing Sean a moment to admire her form. Recognizing his evident approval through the outline in his sweatpants, she proceeded to strip him of his pants as he shed his shirt. Lying back, he watched as she positioned herself atop him, before immediately immersing herself in their union. Her movements began gently, then gained fervor, as she consciously surrendered to the release of her accumulated tension.

As they merged round after round in a whirlwind of movement, it was evident this was not about forging a connection but seeking a diversion. Karyn was chasing a fleeting feeling, anything to distract from the constant anxiety that plagued her. Sean, not privy to her plight, still managed to match her fervor, their silent consensus to find satisfaction in the tactile, where words and feelings were put aside.

Post climax, the room returned to its former stillness. In that quiet aftermath, Karyn cherished the brief escape from her concerns. However, as the fleeting pleasure waned, the Quilt, no doubt an eavesdropper to her escapades, now loomed ominously larger in her thoughts, her earlier defiance ripe in her mind. Her attempt at escaping her reality had underscored her profound entanglement with her family's heritage—a cycle from which sex could never provide a real getaway, only the illusion of such.

The stillness of the night was brutally shattered by an alarming series of sounds, "BOOM! BOOM! BOOM!"—each one more terrifying than the last. The force of the noise sent vibrations through the bed frame, as terror rippled through Karyn's body. She glanced at the other side of her bed, only to find it empty. Sean must have left after she'd dozed off. Realizing she was alone with whatever was in the house, her heart catapulted into a frenzied beat, a primal alertness slicing through the lingering veils of sleep. For a moment, she lay petrified, her breath caught in a tight clutch of fear and confusion. No. Who was she kidding? She knew exactly what the sound was. The Quil t.

With a shaky exhale, Karyn forced herself to move, her limbs heavy with a dread. The cold wood of the floor bit into her feet as she stood, a visceral reminder that this was not a dream. As she took hesitant steps toward the door, her mind raced to potential defenses. But how could she possibly defend herself against the unseen? The journey from her bedroom to the sewing room felt like an odyssey. Each creak of the floorboards under her weight was a shout in the smothering silence. The air was electric, charged with an energy that made the tiny hairs on the back of her neck prickle with dread.

Reaching the door to the sewing room, Karyn paused, her hand hovering over the doorknob. "BOOM! BOOM! BOOM!" The sound came again, this time unmistakably from within the room. Gathering every ounce of courage, Karyn flung the door open, bracing herself for whatever might come. Her eyes immediately darted to the Quilt, but it was still, almost mockingly so.

"Listen, cut the shit. I know that was you! Why can't you just leave me the fuck alone?" she yelled into the room, her words both a challenge and plea. The absurdity of questioning a Quilt wasn't lost on her, yet in the face of the unexplainable, it seemed as reasonable as anything else in her family's history.

In response, The Quilt seemed to smirk at her outburst, its silence a mocking rebuke to her defiance. Karyn's heart pounded fervently as the Quilt remained impassive, its patterns shadowed under the moon's gaze, yet unmistakably taunting.

"I'm not afraid of you," Karyn lied, her voice barely a whisper. "In fact I can show you better than I can tell you." But her bravado was forced. Each step she took towards the Quilt was a battle, her resolve pitted against the screaming instinct to run. Then, just as she reached out a trembling hand to yank the Quilt down, the fabric erupted into a furious life of its own. It flung itself from the wall with a violence that was personal, swirling around Karyn in a whirlwind of fabric and shadow. She barely had time to gasp before it wrapped around her, a constrictor made of patches and stitches, each fold a vise tightening around her.

Karyn struggled, her arms pinned, her breaths coming in sharp, desperate gasps as the fabric pressed against her face, transforming her screams into muffled cries. The world began to spin, the room blurring into a vortex of colors and darkness as the Quilt tightened its embrace.

Panic surged through her, a primal, tearing need for air, for freedom. Her fingers clawed at the fabric, finding no purchase, no gap through which to fight back. The Quilt was alive, its movements deliberate, punishing her for her refusal to comply with its demands.

In that moment, Karyn's mind raced, thoughts fragmented by fear and desperation. Memories of Elaine, her warnings about if she ever failed to uphold her obligations, flashed through her mind. She thought of Sia, of the life she hoped to protect her from, of the choices that had led her to this moment of reckoning with a legacy that demanded blood. But as the struggle continued, Karyn's movements grew weaker, her resistance fading into a desperate acceptance of the inevitable. The room dimmed at the edges, her world narrowing to the suffocating embrace of the Quilt, to the darkness that crept into the edges of her vision, then to a space where there's nothing.

Sunlight softly filtered through the curtains, gently nudging Karyn awake. She stretched in her sewing chair, her body feeling oddly disconnected, as if emerging from a deeper, more distant sleep. "Shit, I must've dozed off," she muttered, her voice tinged with a confusion she couldn't place.

Picking up her phone, she noticed a text from Sean glowing on the screen:

"Hey, beautiful. What you doing?"

A smile attempted to form on Karyn's lips, but it felt strangely foreign.

"Just woke up. Fell asleep at my desk. Working too hard, I guess. Looking forward to the weekend, though."

Sending the message, her eyes drifted to the Quilt. Its colors seemed changed, somehow. A memory flickered at the edge of her mind that wouldn't quite form. "Why does it look so different now?" she whispered, the question hanging unanswered in the air.

"I need coffee," she mumbled, almost automatically heading to the kitchen. The coffee maker hummed to life, but the aroma that filled the room was lackluster, missing the warmth and comfort it usually brought. "Bad batch?" Karyn mused aloud.

As she sipped the coffee, its taste was fine but unremarkable. *Maybe I need a new can*, she thought, setting the cup down.

Her phone vibrated again, drawing her back from her thoughts. It was Sean:

"Something feels different today, doesn't it?"

Karyn paused, a frown creasing her brow. A fleeting memory teased her—but of what, she couldn't place. Shaking her head, she typed, "Different how?" but then erased it, replacing it with a non-committal, "You think so?"

As she waited for Sean's response, the sensation of chasing a half-remembered dream brushed against her thoughts once more. It was disorienting, like glimpses of a life just out of reach.

Sean replied:

"IDK. Maybe it's just me. Enjoy your day…"

Her smile was hesitant, her eyes clouded with confusion. She placed the phone down, her gaze scanning the room. Everything appeared normal, yet there was a dissonance, like a note out of tune.

"I'm just tired… been working too hard," she reasoned, her voice not quite convincing even to herself.

She took another sip of her coffee, thinking, *I really need a vacation*. But even that thought felt alien, as if the desire for escape belonged to someone else's life.

Returning to her sewing room, Karyn sat before the dress she was working on. Usually, the feel of the fabric would ignite a creative fire within her, but now her touch felt numb, devoid of the passion that once defined her.

The sewing machine started with its familiar hum, yet it sounded subtly altered. Lost in a daze, Karyn was startled by the buzz of her phone – a "Rush Order Request" email. She skimmed the details: a complex design, an impossibly tight deadline. The challenge should have been daunting, but today, a strange compulsion gripped her, pushing her to accept. As she immersed herself in her work, the odd sense of displacement persisted, a nagging feeling that something fundamental about her reality had shifted.

Shaking off the unease, Karyn reached for her phone, her fingers hesitating for a moment before she launched into a social media update. "Hey, lovelies," she spoke into the camera, her voice lacking its usual vibrancy, "working on something fabulous for a fave of yours. Stay tuned!" She forced a smile as she hit 'Post', watching the likes and comments flood in, the digital applause feeling oddly distant.

A message from her friend Kalima popped up: "Girl, saw your post. You're always on the grind! When do you even sleep?"

Karyn chuckled, typing back, "Sleep? That's for the weak!" But as she sent it, she felt that same tickle of a memory at the edge of her mind. The memory remained elusive, however, slipping away each time she tried to grasp it.

Returning to her sewing, the fabric glided smoothly under the needle, yet the rhythm of the machine felt even more discordant now. A while later, she updated her followers, trying to sound enthusiastic: "Progress, my lovelies! More to come." But her heart wasn't in it and the words felt rehearsed.

Her gaze shifted to the Quilt and for a split second, it appeared as if a pattern shifted. She blinked, and it was still again. "Get it the fuck together, girl," she whispered to herself.

Another buzz from her phone brought her back. It was Sean:

"Can't wait to see that masterpiece you working on. How about dinner at Davinci's tonight? I want to see you."

A genuine smile this time. "Italian sounds perfect. See you at 7!" she replied, her spirits momentarily lifted.

But as she continued working, that persistent sense of something being off crept back. Her eyes drifted to a framed photo on her desk – her and her late grandmother, their once smiling faces tinged with an indefinable unease. She shook her head, trying to dispel the unsettling feeling. But despite her attempts to focus, the feeling lingered.

As dusk fell, Karyn clipped the final thread, holding up the dress. It really was a master-piece, but the satisfaction she usually felt was undercut by her discomfort. Reaching for her phone, she narrated, "Ta-da, my lovelies! Another creation comes to life," but again, her voice lacked its usual warmth.

Her phone buzzed again: Sean.

"Long day. Starving. Just got off. Can I pick you up at 8?"

She hesitated, the sense of wrongness gnawing at her. Shaking it off again she replied, "8 is fine! See you soon."

As she turned to leave, a faint, almost inaudible whisper emanated from the Quilt. "Karynnn."

She paused, her heart skipping a beat, but the silence quickly returned. Chiding herself for letting her imagination run wild, she left the room, feeling an unexplainable sense of being out of place. Even the sound of her slippers against the hardwood floor seemed strangely loud, a feeling of surrealness engulfing her. In the bathroom, she turned on the shower, the steam enveloping her. The warm water should have been soothing, but it only deepened her sense of disquiet. Frustrated, she finished her shower. As she dried off, her reflection in the mirror appeared changed somehow—her face was mostly the same, but her eyes—they seemed hollow in some way.

Wrapped in her towel, Karyn approached her vanity with a sense of trepidation. She reached for her makeup, her movements mechanical, distant. But as she glanced in the mirror, her heart froze in her chest. Karyn stood frightened in awe as she took in her face—its form twisted grotesquely, her eyes sunken into dark voids, mouth agape in an unnatural grimace, revealing sharp, needle-like teeth. Her skin, now a ghastly gray, was marred by dark, writhing veins. Karyn was staring at a monster.

A sharp gasp shattered the silence, her hand clapping over her mouth in horror. Her fingers shook uncontrollably, almost dropping the foundation bottle. Cold sweat beaded on her forehead, her entire being recoiling from the nightmarish reflection confronting her. She squeezed her eyes shut, willing the horrific vision away. When she dared to look again, her normal reflection stared back, eyes wide with shock and confusion.

"What the hell's happening to me?" she whispered to her reflection.

Deep breaths did little to steady her racing heart. Trembling, she resumed applying her makeup with deliberate strokes, eventually becoming lost in her movements. Suddenly, an alert from her cellphone caused her to jump. It was Sean: "OMW. See you soon!"

A fleeting warmth touched her at Sean's words. She typed back, "Okay. See you soon," her mind still a mix of fear and confusion. Turning from the vanity, Karyn's gaze drifted to the window. The dusky streets outside her home were peaceful, but a little girl's laughter, floating up from somewhere, sparked an unbidden vision of a life imbued with a different kind of joy—a life she couldn't quite remember but felt intimately familiar.

Shrugging it off, she moved to her closet, selecting a sleek black dress. As she slipped it on, the fabric felt strange against her skin, another reminder of the dissonance that clawed at her consciousness. Trying to will off the sensation, she completed her look by securing her favorite hoop earrings and applying a dash of perfume to her neck, wrists, and ankles. After a final glance in the mirror, her reflection appeared complete, but still, something seemed amiss. "Your shoes, Karyn," she reminded herself, letting out a nervous giggle.

Slipping into her heels, she heard the doorbell chime. Excitement mingled with apprehension in her stomach. She grabbed her keys, her cell, and her bag, then glanced in the full-length mirror once more. Satisfied, yet pensive, she headed to meet Sean. At the front door, she took a deep breath to steady her nerves and opened it to Sean's warm, inviting smile. He stood there with a bouquet of white roses in hand.

"Damn, you look good girl," he complimented, his eyes meeting hers before leaning in for a kiss.

"Thanks," she replied, accepting the roses with a half smile. "You're not so bad yourself."

As they walked to his car, the sense of unease within her grew stronger, but she continued to push it aside, determined to focus on the evening ahead.

Inside the car, the soft music and warmth was a drastic contrast to the chill that had settled in Karyn's bones. Sean's voice offered some comfort, but her anxiety remained a silent companion. "How was your day?" he asked, glancing her way.

"Hectic, but good. Rush order on a custom dress," she replied, her voice distant, as if she were talking about someone else's life.

"That's my girl, always booked and busy," Sean said, squeezing her knee. "You're incredible, you know?"

Karyn managed a smile, feeling more like an actor than herself. "Thanks. And how was your day?" she asked.

"Busy, as always. But better now that I'm with you," he said.

As they drove past the local high school, the ambient glow of its lights bathed the car in a soft luminescence, while the distant sounds of a football game carried through the air, infusing the moment with a sense of normalcy and youthful exuberance. The laughter and cheers, the unmistakable energy of high school spirits in full display, wrapped around them, a welcome change to Karyn's off-kilter day.

Then, as sudden as a storm breaking the horizon, an overwhelming realization crashed over Karyn. The joy from the football field, so pure and untainted, became a catalyst for a memory so deep and so painful that it forced a sharp intake of breath from her.

"Sean, pull over! Now!" Her voice, tinged with a desperation Sean had never heard before, cut through the night. Without hesitation, Sean complied, concern etching his features as he brought the car to a stop at the side of the road.

"What's wrong, Karyn? Talk to me!"

Karyn turned to him, her face a mask of dawning horror, tears pooling in her eyes as if the floodgates had been opened. "It's all wrong... I remember something... oh my god."

I lost her, Sean. My daughter... I think she's been taken from me!" The words tumbled out, each one laden with a weight that seemed to crush the air around them.

Memories, once suppressed, surged forward in Karyn's mind with a clarity that was both vivid and haunting. She recalled the ritual she had defiantly refused to perform, the moment the Quilt had wrapped its fabric around her, punishing her refusal. But now, another memory surfaced, one that twisted the knife of guilt and loss deeper into her heart—a life she had forgotten, a daughter she once had... Sia. The realization that she might have lost her daughter, not to the world but to the insidious demands of her family's curse, was a revelation that shattered her composure.

As Sean took in Karyn's devastation, his expression was a mix of concern, confusion, and fear. "We need to get you home, Karyn. This is a lot."

Karyn met his gaze, her eyes revealing a haunting realization. "Sean. I remember now. What I've lost... no... what was stolen from me. I have to fix this. This life... it's not mine. All of this is wrong... even us. Since when do we go on dates, Sean?"

The drive back was blanketed in silence, the once comforting music now discordant. Sean's occasional glances were filled with an awkward unease, as if he were sitting beside a stranger. Karyn's hands twisted anxiously in her lap, her mind struggling to reconcile with the reality that was crumbling around her. Each streetlight cast her in a transient spotlight, revealing the raw fear etched on her face.

Arriving at her house, Sean parked the car, the engine idling. Karyn's breaths were shallow, as she battled against the constriction in her chest. "Will you come in with me?" she whispered, her voice fragile.

Sean nodded, his face lined with worry. They ascended the porch together, their footsteps sounding against the wood ominously. At her door, Karyn's trembling hands fumbled with the keys before unlocking it. Stepping inside, they were greeted by an air of change. Hesitantly, Sean followed Karyn to the sewing room, where the Quilt pulsed in the dim light.

"Would you like a drink?" Karyn offered nervously.

"A drink? No. Are you okay, Karyn?" Sean's voice shook, his eyes searching hers for answers. "Something feels very wrong."

But before Karyn could reply, the Quilt emitted a guttural sound, its fabric contorting wildly.

"What the fuck is that?" Sean staggered back, his voice laced with fear.

"The Celestial Quilt," Karyn whispered, trembling.

As they stood transfixed, the Quilt underwent a sinister metamorphosis, its elaborate patterns bending and weaving together to form a shadowy, human-like silhouette. A voice then permeated the air, tainted with an otherworldly malevolence. "I am Dúr, the keeper of pacts and devourer of destinies," it proclaimed, the fabric undulating as if to give form to its words. "Your ancestor, Alice, stood before me as you do now, desperate and seeking longevity and prosperity for her lineage. In exchange for the prosperity she so craved, a pact was struck, binding her and her descendants to me through blood and sacrifice."

The voice grew colder, its tone sharpening with a palpable rage. "Now you have dared to defy our covenant. You denied me the sustenance I am owed, dishonoring not just our agreement but the very lineage that you are part of."

Suddenly, the Quilt's voice escalated, filling the room with its fury. "For your insolence, you will be obliterated from existence, your essence devoured as restitution for the debt unpaid! I will consume every fragment of your being, reclaiming what was promised to me! You and all traces of your defiance will be expunged, as if you never were!"

The Quilt's declaration sent a shiver down Karyn's spine, its words echoing like a death knell. In a last-ditch effort, Karyn's voice broke through the thickening dread, "Please, isn't there any mercy? Any forgiveness for not understanding the full weight of this all?" But her plea dissipated into the void, met with silence from the entity before her.

As the room darkened further, specters of her ancestors began to materialize, forming a circle of judgment around her. Their faces, etched with centuries of sorrow and resignation, turned towards Karyn, their gazes piercing her very soul. Among them, Alice and Elaine stood prominently, their expressions particularly inscrutable.

Driven by desperation, Karyn confronted Alice, the matriarch whose decision had ensnared their lineage. "Why? Why bind us to such a horrific fate? Was there truly no other way?" her voice trembled, seeking answers from the spectral figure before her.

Alice, silent and unyielding, offered no comfort or explanation, her gaze as distant and removed as if she were separated by an abyss of time and choice. Feeling abandoned by her own blood, Karyn turned frantically to Sean, hoping for an anchor in this storm of despair. But Sean was horror stricken— frozen in place with fear.

Then, as if yanked from his fright, Sean yelled, "Karyn, look! Behind you!"

Karyn spun around just in time to see the Quilt flying toward her with an unnatural speed. Then, one one by one, the Quilt began to stretch out its threads like tentacles, latching onto her body in a grotesque embrace. Piece by piece, the Quilt leached away Karyn's very essence. Her figure blurred, edges fraying into nothingness as the Quilt rendered her threadbare, each thread dragging her soul, her memories, her very existence into its depths, until nothing remained.

Sean collapsed to the floor, his mind reeling in disbelief. He fumbled for his phone, his fingers shaking, as he dialed 911. But then he stopped, realizing the futility. How could he explain what had just happened? Defeated, Sean rose and staggered out of the house, the door clicking shut behind him. As he made his way to his car, a deep sense of horror and loss engulfed him.

As time passed, the house gradually faded into obscurity, leaving only the Quilt in its wake. It now exists in a realm caught between life, death, and rebirth—its essence intertwined with Karyn's memory, a memory that Sean alone carries, suspended in the timeless void.

ZONE ELEVEN: PART II

THE ANCHOR

Aja Jones kneeled in her garden, her hands painted in soil and sweat. "Y'all ever think about how plants just do their thing, reaching out for what they need, no matter what's going on around them?" Aja asked, facing her camera. Her followers responded with a flurry of comments, hearts, and thumbs-up icons cascading down her screen. She paused her monologue to the unseen eyes glued to her live stream, and tilted her camera toward a patch of basil.

Just as she was about to dive deeper into her thoughts on plants and resilience, a sound—a crunch of gravel—pulled her attention away. Three sharply dressed figures, a woman and two men, incongruous against the backdrop of her garden, came into view. Aja stood, her usual ease replaced by a hint of cautious interest.

"Miss. Jones? Miss. Aja Jones?" The woman, draped in a black suit approached with a natural authority. Her skin, a rich brown, contrasted beautifully with her attire, her cropped and coiled hair accentuating high cheekbones and hazel, almond shaped eyes, enhancing her composed yet imposing presence.

"I am," Aja affirmed, maintaining her composure while eyeing the phone still live streaming. "Can I help you?"

The woman extended a hand and introduced herself, "I'm Dr. Regina Reyes, and these are my colleagues, Agents Robert Marino and Leon Finch, but you can call me Regina. We're from the Agency of Interstellar Affairs, and yes, actually I think you can help me."

"Oh, yeah? How so?" Aja asked, curiously.

"We're here because of your online presence Miss. Jones. Your work with the earth and how you engage with your plants—it's extraordinary to say the least."

Aja exhaled, her skepticism clear. "Is this about me pissing off pharmaceutical companies because I'm offering natural remedies that undercut their profits?" She glanced at her live feed. "Y'all see this shit?"

"No, Ms. Jones, that's not it," Regina assured her. "We're here because of your unique talents. We need your expertise."

Agent Finch added, "I'll be frank, Miss. Jones. We're at a critical juncture, facing a cosmic threat. If we can't avert it, we might have to relocate humanity—or at least some of humanity. There's a newly discovered planet half a light year away that's ideal for a fresh start. Your skills in nurturing the earth are crucial for making it habitable."

Aja's initial amusement waned as the gravity of their words settled in. "You're serious? You want me to help terraform a new planet because I know a thing or two about growing plants?"

"Exactly," confirmed Regina, locking eyes with Aja to underscore the sincerity of their request. "Your knowledge in cultivating life is invaluable. You've built a community here; imagine the possibilities elsewhere."

Aja pondered their proposition. Could she trust the government, given its track record on Earth?

"How can I be sure this is legitimate and not some trick or experiment? Cuz I know how y'all like to experiment on Black folk..."

"We can't share everything publicly," Agent Marino explained with a nod to Aja's livestream setup, "but the danger to Earth is urgent and genuine. This is about securing humanity's future and I can assure you the only experiment would be the seeds you'd bring to this new planet to determine if it's habitable for us."

Aja looked at her phone, a mix of angry and awestruck emojis flooding her screen. "And if I agree? What, I just take my gardening tools to space?"

Regina smiled. "There's more to it—training, preparations. But essentially, yes. You'll help us make the planet thrive, using your intimate understanding of nature."

The conversation unfolded, questions met with answers, fears with reassurances. But, Aja's followers, though silent, were a comforting presence.

"Mannn... I don't know about this. This is some wild shit. I'ma need some time to think," Aja stated.

Regina offered an empathetic look. "Aja—we get that this is very much out of the ordinary, and we understand the gravity of such a decision. It's not asked of you lightly."

Agent Finch, his demeanor softened by understanding, added, "Please consider quickly, though. We're racing against time."

"I understand, but it's just that y'all want me to just up and leave everything. My life, my community... my father..."

Regina approached her, resting a hand lightly on Aja's forearm, giving a knowing look. "Hey, Sis. Believe me, I know how you're feeling. And I promise—we'll support you in every way. However, if you care for your family and your community the way I know you do... you'll give it some serious consideration. We're doing this for us."

Aja absorbed Regina's assurances. "I hear you," she affirmed, "...and I'll think it over. But if I do agree... it'll be on my terms. You a sista and all, but you also work for them," she said, with a nod to the other agents.

"That's all we ask," Regina said with a gentle smile.

As the trio prepared to leave, Regina subtly pointed a small gadget at Aja's phone. A quiet zap followed, and instantly, Aja's live feed—and their entire conversation—was wiped clean.

"What the—" Aja began, frustration bubbling up. "Did you just kill my stream? See... that's the shit I'm talking about..."

"For national security reasons," Regina explained, her tone laced with a mix of apology and firmness. "Your phone's alright, but our discussion needs to stay between us. Your viewers will forget, but you'll remember."

A whirlwind of emotions hit Aja—irritation, shock, and a spark of curiosity. But, watching the group disappear, what lingered for Aja wasn't just the strangeness of their encounter, but a profound sense of disbelief. "What the hell just happened?"

Later that day, dinner unfolded in silence, the kitchen filled with the comforting aromas of fried chicken, complemented by the sweetness of baked yams and the hearty fragrance of Aja's garden grown collard greens. James, Aja's father, interrupted the silence.

"Aja, you've been quieter than the moon tonight. What's on your mind, baby girl?"

Aja poked at her food, the flavors she usually savored now tasteless. "Dad... some people visited me today... from the government," she replied, the words feeling surreal on her tongue.

James chuckled, "Government folks? Here? What'd they want? Tell you to stop talking to the plants?"

"No, Dad. They... they want me to help terraform a new planet." Aja's voice was steady, but her heart raced.

"A new planet? Aja, are you sure you didn't smoke something funny from that garden of yours?"

"I'm serious, Dad." Aja met his gaze. "They said I could help make it a home. Because of my... connection to the earth. Because of what Mama taught me."

James leaned back, his skepticism softening into contemplation. "Your mama was a special soul, Aja. Had a way with the earth I've never seen. But this... this is beyond anything..."

"I know, Dad. It's... wild. But what if it's true? What if I can do something? What if this is my chance to make a difference, not just here, but out there?" Aja's words tumbled out.

James studied his daughter, the fire of her mother's spirit alive in her eyes. "Aja, your mama always said we're stewards of this earth. But another planet? That's a big leap from tending to our homestead."

Aja nodded. "It is. And I haven't said yes. But Dad, what if this is what I'm meant to do? Carry on Mama's legacy, but on a scale we never imagined?"

Silence settled between them, the kitchen clock ticking away the moments of uncertainty. Finally, James spoke, his voice softer, "If there's anyone who could do it, Aja, it's you. Your mama would be proud... I think," he smiled. "Just... promise me you'll be careful. This government of ours... they haven't exactly been kind to *this* planet. I can't say I have much faith in what they'll do with another one."

Aja's hand met her father's across the table. "I'll be cautious, Dad. And I'll give it serious thought."

Their conversation gently shifted away, yet Aja's thoughts lingered on the monumental choice before her. Post-dinner, she was drawn to the porch, gazing at the stars, each a light to unknown worlds.

Is leaving everything I know behind possible? she mused, the enormity of the decision pressing on her. *Can I extend Mama's legacy beyond our world?*

The night's stillness enveloped her as she contemplated the magnitude of her potential role.

Later that evening, sleep eluded Aja, and in the profound stillness that only deep night can bring, she found herself rising from bed at 3AM. It was that peculiar hour when moments seem to hang in the balance, tethered neither to the day past or the day to come. Guided by a mix of restlessness and purpose, she made her way to her altar. In this serene corner, Aja always found peace.

The altar, its surface draped in a white cloth, held an array of items: photographs capturing smiles of generations past, personal mementos from transitioned relatives, alongside shot glasses filled with liquor, a clear glass brimming with water, and an assortment of candies and cigars. Each piece told a story, inviting the whispers of ancestors into the space. Aja remembered standing here as a little girl, her mother's hand guiding hers, introducing her to each item, imbuing her with the wisdom of their lineage. That tender memory, filled with her mother's love and the silent counsel of their forebears, steadied Aja now as she sought answers amidst the chaos swirling in her mind.

Aja reached for her lighter and then ignited the wick of a white candle, observing as its flame danced, its shadow flickering against the walls of the darkened room. She inhaled deeply, the air filled with a mix of excitement and a hint of camphor from the day before.

"I welcome the presence of my elevated ancestors—both known and unknown," Aja's voice, steady yet imbued with reverence, broke the silence. "I ask for your presence now. Mama. I need your help especially. Please... guide my path."

With a practiced hand, Aja took up five divination coins—quarters, worn by time and touch. The ritual was familiar, yet tonight it held the weight of her future, of countless futures.

Closing her eyes, Aja focused on her question, the very essence of her dilemma. "Is it my path to bring my gifts to another planet?" She could feel the energy around her, a subtle shift in the air, as the spirits drew near.

Breathing out slowly, Aja tossed the coins on the altar, entrusting her question to her ancestors' insight. The coins came to rest with gentle clinks upon the cloth, their positions revealing an answer from beyond.

One by one, she counted—heads, heads, heads, heads, and heads again. A resounding yes. All five coins, a unanimous chorus from the spirits, affirming her path.

For good measure, she divined again... and once again, a resounding yes was the response.

Aja sighed as a wave of emotion washed over her. The message was clear, unequivocal. Her ancestors, her mother's spirit among them, had spoken.

The candle flickered in approval, its light a comforting embrace. As Aja stood in silence, she allowed the significance of the moment to settle around her. "Asé." she said bowing her head. "Mama, family, thank you for showing me the way."

Khalil Brown flipped the sign to 'Open' on the door of his metaphysical shop, Conjure Corner, letting the early morning light wash over the eclectic collection of mystical wares. As he straightened a display of quartz crystals, his thoughts drifted towards his ex, Kia, and the recent end of their relationship. It had been mutual, both agreeing their paths were veering in different directions, yet her disclosure that she'd been unhappy with him for some time still troubled him.

He chuckled to himself, shaking his head. "Always easier to read others than read myself," he mused, finding a wry amusement in the irony. His gifts allowed him to peer into the lives of his clients, offering clarity and guidance, yet his own life's path seemed wrapped in a fog he couldn't quite penetrate.

Lately, his dreams had been vivid—a mix of foreboding and promise, hinting at something monumental on the horizon, but something awful as well. He often wondered if the universe was teasing him with riddles or preparing him for a pivotal role in something beyond Philadelphia. His ability to navigate the mysteries of others' lives with ease, contrasted starkly with the questions that danced just out of reach in his own.

The chime of the door pulled Khalil from his thoughts, and he looked up to see three people stepping into his shop. Everything about them screamed 'federal government'; louder than a bullhorn at a library, an amusing contrast to the shop's more laid back vibe.

"Good morning. Welcome to Conjure Corner, where the magick happens—literally," Khalil greeted them with a grin. "How can I help y'all tap in today?"

The woman leading the group, held an air of authority softened by genuine curiosity, as she stepped forward. "Good morning, Mr. Brown. I'm Dr. Regina Reyes and these are my colleagues, Agent Finch and Agent Marino. We're here on behalf of the Agency of Interstellar Affairs. But, it's not the universe we're looking to understand today... it's you."

Khalil raised an eyebrow, his interest piqued. "The Agency of Interstellar Affairs? I must say, you're a long way from home. My expertise usually involves tarot, not telescopes. What brings y'all to my little corner of the cosmos?"

Regina smiled slightly, acknowledging the humor. "We're here because we believe you have a particular set of skills that could be vital to a mission we're undertaking. It's... unconventional, to say the least."

Khalil leaned on the counter, the playful twinkle in his eye giving way to keen interest. "Unconventional is my middle name. Tell me more. And just for the record, if this is about saving the world, I do have a cape, but it's at the dry cleaners."

The agents exchanged amused glances, before delving into the details of their visit. As they spoke of Zone Eleven, the cloaked planet, and the role they hoped he would play, Khalil listened, his humor making way for the realization that the dreams and the sense of anticipation that had been building might have found their anchor in reality.

By the time they concluded, Khalil found himself both bemused and intrigued by the path that seemed to be unfurling before him—and he'd already made his decision. "Well, Dr. Reyes, it looks like the universe has a sense of humor after all. But, okay, I'm wit it. I only ask for one thing ... aside from a nice compensation package of course."

"And what is that, Mr. Brown?" Regina replied, amused.

"Just make sure there's coffee... I'ma need a lot of it. Like a lot, a lot."

After a steep descent into the pits of Midtown Atlanta, Aja exited the elevator and crossed the threshold into AIA headquarters, immediately spotting Regina in the reception area. A tall, brown complexioned man, with kind eyes stood next to Regina. He was nice looking, wearing casual clothing— jeans and a t-shirt—but there was a certain air about him that tickled her senses— literally. Shaking off the feeling, Aja walked over to the pair, and Regina quickly facilitated introductions. "Hi, Aja, I'm so happy you're here! This is Khalil Brown. Like you, he has a profound metaphysical insight that's essential for our journey," Regina said, gesturing towards Khalil who offered a friendly nod.

"Hi, Aja. Nice to meet you," he said, extending his hand.

Oh, so that's what that was? He a magickal negro, Aja thought, as her hand met his. "Nice to meet you, Khalil."

Later, as they settled into the conference room's relaxed atmosphere, Aja seized the moment to connect with Khalil a little deeper—the earlier tingle she felt still brushing against her mind. "So, Khalil, how do you really feel about all this?"

Khalil grinned, his eyes gleaming with a mix of humor and insight. "Honestly? I kinda feel like we've been drafted into the universe's most ambitious crossover episode. Think about it, we're about to dive headfirst into the great cosmic unknown, with a side mission of inter-galactic healing. It's like being in a sci-fi movie, only the special effects are real."

Aja laughed, feeling an immediate kinship. "Right. Like, I'm all for connecting with Earth, but this? Extending that connection beyond our planet feels wild... no... actually it's terrifying."

Khalil nodded, his smile broadening. "But for me, it's the thrill of the unknown that made me say yes. Plus... a free vacation and a fat compensation package. Yeah, I'll take it— especially since I doubt we finna get any real reparations any time soon."

Their laughter filled the room, easing the weight of the mission ahead.

A few moments later, their conversation was gently paused as Regina called the room to order. "Good morning everyone. Before we dive into today's agenda, there's crucial information you all need to understand," she began, ensuring she had everyone's attention. "Our guide in all of this, a tech-based entity named S.O.P.H.I.A., has unveiled significant details about what we're up against—Zone Eleven. It's not just a potential threat; it's an imminent threat to humanity's existence. We're talking *Endgame*— but in real life."

Aja, her brows knitting together, chimed in, "S.O.P.H.I.A.? Could you elaborate on that and Zone Eleven for us?"

"Absolutely," Regina affirmed. "S.O.P.H.I.A. isn't just any intel source. She's brought us face-to-face with cosmic phenomena beyond our comprehension. Zone Eleven is, for lack of a better term, a cosmic devourer—erasing not just matter, but the essence of reality itself. Against it, our usual tech and tactics are virtually ineffective."

Khalil leaned forward, intrigued. "And about this cloaked planet? How does it fit into the equation?"

Regina spread her hands on the table, grounding the gravity of their discussion. "This planet represents our leap into the unknown. According to S.O.P.H.I.A., it's habitable yet enshrouded in secrecy, suggesting its hidden nature is a deliberate safeguard against entities just like Zone Eleven."

"So, our mission is to decode this planet's mysteries? Specifically, me and Khalil?" Aja asked.

"Exactly," Regina confirmed with a nod. "We're to uncover everything—the ecosystem, its level of sentience, its viability for human life, and any other secrets it holds. It appears S.O.P.H.I.A. believes this planet has protective qualities we need to understand from a metaphysical perspective."

Aja and Khalil exchanged a knowing glance.

Next, the conversation shifted towards T.E.S.S., the ship's Tactical Environmental Support System. The lead engineer, Mike Chen, spoke with a blend of awe and reverence. "T.E.S.S. transcends mere navigation. It's our protector, our guide, and essentially, our guardian across the cosmos. Thanks to S.O.P.H.I.A., we're equipped with the most sophisticated tech in existence—algorithms that adapt in real-time, environmental controls to maintain stability, all designed to ensure we thrive in the unpredictable vastness of s pace."

His enthusiasm grew as he detailed its capabilities. "This system is prepped for the myriad challenges of space. It manages our life support, deciphers alien atmospheres, and steps in during emergencies to safeguard us. Essentially, T.E.S.S. acts as the mission's brain, continuously monitoring, adapting, and ensuring our wellbeing. It's our guide and safety net in the uncharted wilderness of space."

After the briefing, Aja and Khalil headed toward the break room. After grabbing a few snacks and a bottle of water, she walked over to join Khalil who was seated with a cup of coffee.

"So, I don't know about you, but I definitely didn't have 'interstellar adventure' on my bingo card this year," Aja said as she settled into her seat.

"Yeah , me neither," Sean smiled. "Seems like the universe decided to play a wildcard on us."

Aja laughed, shaking her head. "A wildcard? Nawl. Try an entire deck. The universe ain't playing games—it's rewriting the rulebook."

Leaning in, Khalil's tone carried both jest and awe. "But think of the tales we'll spin, Aja. We won't just be star travelers; we'll be pioneers, part of a narrative that'll redefine the world's understanding of the universe."

Aja's laughter softened into a thoughtful smile. "Yeah, but it's still a lot, isn't it? Being thrust into a saga that's quite literally astronomical. But I do see how our gifts, our essence, could very well forge a new path for humanity."

"Exactly," Khalil affirmed, their gazes locking in mutual respect and a burgeoning sense of partnership. "It's a testament to our unique perspectives. We're not just participants; we're at the heart of discovery, embodying the belief that our connections to life extend beyond our blue dot."

As they parted for the day, Aja carried with her the depth of Khalil's reflections. The task ahead was indeed formidable, beckoning them to tap into their most profound abilities. But Khalil's words lingered—a gentle reminder of the honor and responsibility they shouldered. The question was—could she rise to the occasion? Time would tell, but for now, Aja felt a flicker of readiness, buoyed by the bond forming between her and Khalil, potential allies in the greatest adventure of their lives.

The eve of their departure stirred a whirlwind of emotions within Khalil as he prepped for the crew's final Earthside rendezvous at a local pub. More than the anticipation of the imminent launch, Khalil's excitement buzzed around spending laid-back moments with Aja outside of HQ. The kinship they'd nurtured had blossomed into a connection he couldn't quite box away into mere friendship. Their shared beliefs and spirited discussions had unknowingly formed a complex, captivating bond.

Checking his reflection, Khalil's mind drifted to a recent heart-to-heart with Aja that had left a distinct mark. Their conversation had danced around the interplay of humanity and Earth, sparking an energetic exchange of insights. It was in these moments, watching Aja's animated expressions, her eyes shimmering with fervor, that Khalil felt the contours of their relationship shifting.

Initially, he'd been struck by her beauty—slim, but curvy and petite, her flawless chestnut skin, complimented by her large, intuitive eyes, that seemed to peer into his soul were the first to captivate him. But the deepness of her dimples brought out by the sound of her laughter, honest and full of life, easily breached his defenses, and her playful banter about the cosmos had a charm he found irresistible. Describing herself as "an interstellar gardener with a knack for cosmic punchlines," she had him laughing heartily, a sound that had been foreign for far too long before meeting her.

It was in this warmth of their shared jests and profound dialogue, Khalil recognized the depth of his affection for her. This realization was both a thrill and a quandary—exhilarating in its rarity, but daunting in its implications for their tightly-knit crew.

Driving to the pub, courtesy of the AIA's temporary arrangements, Khalil wrestled with his intent to keep things strictly professional with Aja, despite the magnetic pull towards something deeper. He acknowledged the mission's primacy, the essential clear-headedness and unity it demanded, yet Aja's spirited presence haunted his thoughts, challenging his resolve.

As Khalil's car came to a stop in front of the pub, an unnerving vision crashed into his thoughts. A vivid image of their destination planet, not serene and welcoming, but cloaked in crimson. Overwhelmed, he lingered in the silence of his vehicle, grappling with the implications of what he'd seen. Finally, with a heavy heart and a sense of urgency propelling him, he exited the car and made his way through the lively atmosphere of the pub, seeking out Regina.

Finding her, Khalil's voice carried a weight that cut through the ambient noise, "Hey, Regina, can we step aside? I need to talk to you privately."

Regina, detecting the seriousness in his tone, nodded and led him to a quiet corner. "What's on your mind, Khalil?"

Without hesitation, Khalil shared his disturbing premonition. "I had a vision... our destination planet, it was... it was covered in blood. This doesn't feel right. Are we sure about the safety of this place?"

Regina's response was immediate and reassuring, yet Khalil couldn't help but detect a sliver of doubt in her voice. "S.O.P.H.I.A.'s conducted thorough checks, Khalil. Everything points to the planet being safe for us," she stated, though her eyes briefly flickered with an uncertainty that Khalil couldn't ignore.

Torn between his gut feeling and the excitement that enveloped the mission, Khalil wrestled with his unease. Opting not to cast a shadow over the evening's high spirits, he retreated into his own thoughts, isolating himself from the group at the bar. With a drink in hand, he remained an observer, his mind stuck on the haunting vision of a world covered in blood, silently questioning the journey ahead.

After her talk with Khalil, Regina stepped outside, needing some fresh air, and a little quiet to make a phone call. Her thoughts lingered on Sean, her brother, who had been found days after his strange call, wandering aimlessly and speaking incoherently, a shell of his former self. Now, with him placed in a mental health facility, she dialed the number for one last check-in before her departure.

Nurse Jenkins, who had shown a particular fondness for Sean, answered the call. "Good evening. Peachtree Holistic Wellness Center. This is Nurse Jenkins, how can I help you?"

"Hi, Nurse Jenkins, it's Regina. I'm calling because I'm going to be away for a while, and I wanted to see how Sean's doing before I leave. Any changes?"

"He's been stable, Regina," Nurse Jenkins replied gently. "Still quite introspective, often mumbling to himself. It's hard to reach him sometimes."

Regina pressed for more details. "Has he mentioned anything specific? Anything that could let us know what triggered all of this?"

"Actually, yes," Nurse Jenkins said thoughtfully. "He keeps talking about 'the shadow beyond the stars.' It's quite specific, repeats it like a mantra. Does that mean anything to you?"

A shiver ran through Regina. Sean's words seemed almost prophetic given her mission, yet she couldn't reveal its nature. "No, it's just... puzzling. Please, just make sure he's comfortable. I'll be away for some time and you won't be able to contact me, but our parents will step in if anything's needed. Keep them posted on any changes, please."

"Will do, Regina. Oh, and he did have a moment of clarity today—smiled briefly. It was good to see. We're here for him, don't worry."

"Thank you, truly. Please take good care of him," Regina responded, her voice laced with gratitude and worry.

"Don't worry, Regina. And remember to take care of yourself as well. Sean's in good hands here."

Ending the call, Regina felt an unsettling connection between Sean's words and her upcoming journey. "... shadow beyond the stars," she repeated to herself, the phrase embedding itself in her thoughts as she headed into the bar. *Whatever's beyond the stars—I hope they have answers for you, Sean.*

In the quiet of her bedroom, illuminated only by the soft glow of a bedside lamp, Aja meticulously packed her belongings, her focus primarily on the selection of herbs and seeds. Each one was chosen not just for its practical utility but also for its spiritual significance, forming a bridge between the earthly and the ethereal. She carefully selected basil for its protective aura; lavender, a symbol of peace and healing; rosemary, for memory and protection; mint, for health and vitality; thyme, embodying bravery; and wheat, symbolizing sustenance and new beginnings, among others for her journey.

As she packed, her thoughts drifted back to earlier at the pub—their pre-mission gathering. The unusual distance in Khalil's demeanor and Regina's subtle, underlying tension hadn't escaped her notice. Their interactions, usually marked by warmth and openness, had been tinged with an unspoken unease. Aja's intuitive nature picked up on these undercurrents immediately, a gentle reminder of the uncertainties that lay ahead.

With the packing done, Aja turned her attention to a ritual of protection—a ritual meant to anchor her to her home and ensure her safety, no matter the cosmic distances. Sitting at her desk, she tore a small piece of paper from a brown paper bag, then took a black marker from the drawer. Focusing her intentions, she penned a petition, a heartfelt invocation for protection, guidance, and a safe return. Over top the invocation, she drew an image of an anchor. When she was done, she folded the petition toward her four times, rotating the paper counter clockwise between each fold, then signed her name on the top f old.

Moving to the kitchen, Aja prepared an herbal concoction, blending Himalayan pink salt with a selection of protective herbs, each adding its energy to the mix. She poured the mixture into a small mason jar, inserted the petition into the mixture, then screwed the lid, before heading out to her garden.

Beneath the moon's watchful eye, Aja chose a spot in her garden where the earth felt welcoming, where the energy hummed with a familiar warmth. With care, she lit a white tea candle on top of the lid, then sat in quiet meditation as the flame flickered in the moonlight. When the flame finally flickered out, and the wax had melted into a protective seal over the lid, she buried the jar, her hands firm yet gentle against the cool soil. "Protect me as I travel beyond this earth, and guide me back home when my work is done," she intoned as she covered the hole, the gravity of the ritual grounding her.

The garden, her sanctuary, felt alive with whispered blessings as she completed the ritual. Standing there, Aja felt a surge of resolve, a sense of preparedness enveloping her. The ritual wasn't just a plea for safety; it was a declaration of her readiness to face the unknown, armed with the strength of her ancestors and the vibrancy of the earth itself.

In her room, concerns for Khalil and Regina shifted into a broader reflection on the journey ahead. Aja's intuition, always a guiding light, felt sharper than ever. It had steered her through the garden ritual, reinforcing her belief in its power to navigate the mission's unseen challenges. As she drifted to sleep, comforted by her Ancestors' protective embrace, Aja trusted that they would also help knit the crew closer, safeguarding their collective purpose.

The next day, Aja and her father arrived at the secluded launchsite, having landed after a short flight from Atlanta less than an hour prior. The moment had arrived— it was time to say goodbye.

"Can't believe my little girl's headed to the stars," James said, his voice thick with emotion as they stood near the entrance of the launch center.

Aja turned to face him. "Dad, I wouldn't be here without you. All those nights stargazing, you feeding my curiosity... it led me here."

James beamed, his voice carrying a mix of pride and concern, "Just make sure you come back with some incredible stories, okay? And stay safe out there."

"I will, Dad. I'll even snag a piece of the cosmos for you," Aja assured him, wrapping him in a heartfelt hug.

Their goodbye was bittersweet, marked by words of encouragement and a few shed tears, as Aja stepped forward into her new chapter alone.

Crossing into the launch facility, Aja was greeted by the sight of her team. Through the grind of rigorous training, these faces had grown familiar, morphing from mere acquaintances into her space-bound kin.

Mike Chen, the chief engineer, chuckled at something on his device, pushing his glasses up in a habitual gesture. His humor and quick-witted solutions had quickly made him a cornerstone of their team.

Leo Barnett, their navigator, alongside Emma Torres, the geologist, and James Park and Lila Nguyen, both skilled engineers, were engaged in light conversation. Charles Toussaint, the culinary wizard of the crew, was animatedly discussing a new dish with Jasmine Rodriguez, their medical lead. And then there was Regina and Khalil, both whom Aja had forged deep connections with. Mingling with the crew, sharing last embraces and words of support, the unity among them was palpable. They were more than a team; they were pioneers on the brink of humanity's boldest journey, each member vital to their collective success.

"Alright, team, this is it," Regina said, gathering them close. "We've trained for this moment, faced every challenge head-on. Remember, we're not just a crew; we're a family. Let's look out for each other out there."

Nods and murmurs of agreement filled the group. As they moved towards the launch pad, Aja took one last look back, carrying with her the hopes and dreams of everyone who had supported her journey, her father's face foremost in her mind. Later, positioned near Khalil as they strapped in, through the soft static of her suit's mic, Aja reached out, "You okay, Khalil?"

His response, a nod seen through the reflection on his visor, carried an undertone of uncertainty that didn't escape Aja. But, before she could probe further, the countdown commenced, a chorus of numbers marking the threshold between Earth and the stars.

"Three, two, one…" T.E.S.S. echoed, heralding the beginning of their odyssey.

The launch was an exhilarating fusion of power and precision. The craft vibrated with the raw energy of its engines coming to life, a tangible roar that gripped the very core of Aja's being. She felt herself pressed into her seat as the spacecraft surged upwards, piercing the atmosphere with determined velocity. Outside, the blue of the sky blended into the black of space, a transition as symbolic as it was physical.

Khalil's hand found hers as the world they knew shrank away, leaving behind a planet they vowed to return to. As the craft broke free from Earth's gravitational embrace, the silence of space enveloped them, a vast calm that contrasted sharply with the chaos of departure. The stars, once distant points of light, now surrounded them in a panoramic spectacle of the universe's vast beauty.

As they catapulted far beyond the only realm she'd ever known, Aja was humbled. *I'm on my way. I'm really on my way.*

Five months later… or so…

Khalil's eyes snapped open, roused by a commotion outside of his quarters. Unlike the expected silence or the routine hum of the spacecraft, the air was alive with sounds of excitement and hurried footsteps echoing through the narrow corridors.

"What's happening?" Aja whispered in the bed beside him.

Khalil, equally puzzled but buoyed by the infectious energy, shrugged. "Let's find out," he suggested, a spark of adventure lighting his eyes.

They dressed quickly, their movements synchronized in the familiarity of routine and shared purpose. They stepped out together, their relationship strengthened by the stars. It was no secret how close they'd become.

The corridor was abuzz, crew members moving briskly towards the main deck, their faces lit with a mix of wonder and disbelief. Aja and Khalil joined the flow, their steps quickening with anticipation.

As they entered the common area, the source of the excitement was immediately apparent. The large viewing screen displayed a breathtaking sight: a swirling vortex of colors, hanging like a cosmic masterpiece against the backdrop of space.

"We've reached the stargate!" Jasmine exclaimed.

Aja's heart leapt at the sight, its beauty and mystery invoking a sense of infinite possibilities. Khalil squeezed her hand as they gazed in awe at the stargate.

"Alright, everyone. Let's prepare for transit," Regina's voice commanded attention, her presence at the helm both reassuring and authoritative. "This is what we've trained for. Let's make history."

The crew took their positions in their seats and strapped in, the spacecraft edging closer to the stargate. The hum of the engines deepened, resonating with the energy pulsating from the vortex.

As they approached the threshold, the spacecraft shuddered, a sensation unlike any they had experienced. A brilliant light enveloped them, and for a moment, time seemed to still.

Then, with a sudden lurch, they were through, the stargate propelling them into the unknown. The view outside transformed dramatically, stars streaking past in a dizzying dance of light and shadow.

"We did it," Khalil whispered into his mic, his voice tinged with wonder and a hint of apprehension for what lay ahead.

Aja nodded, her gaze fixed on the void beyond, "Yes, we did," she affirmed.

Moments later, unstrapped from their seats, the cloaked planet unfolded beneath them, a palette of greens and blues, painting a picture of tranquility from the spacecraft's viewport. Aja couldn't help but let a soft "Wow' escape her lips, her eyes reflecting the planet's vibrant hues.

"Looks like paradise," Mike remarked from behind her.

Aja turned to him, her smile broadening. "Let's hope it's not just a facade," she said, her gaze drifting back to the view outside.

The landing was smooth, a testament to T.E.S.S's engineering prowess. Once the engines powered down, drones were sent out to test the environment. Upon their return, and after T.E.S.S. gave the okay, the crew gathered at the airlock, anticipation buzzing through the air like static.

"Alright, team," Regina began, her voice commanding yet filled with excitement. "Remember, we don't know what awaits us out there. Stay alert, stay together."

The airlock hissed open, revealing the alien landscape in all its glory. The atmosphere was breathable, a gentle breeze carrying the scent of unfamiliar flora.

"Feels like Earth," Leo observed, taking a deep breath.

Aja led the way, her boots making soft impressions on the soil. The ground was covered in a carpet of moss-like vegetation, spongy underfoot. She knelt, running her fingers through the greenery, a sense of connection flowing through her.

"This... feels right," she murmured to herself.

The exploration team ventured further, their path winding through towering trees with iridescent leaves. The sound of a distant watercourse sounded somewhere in the distance— the promise of discovery of a river or stream, urging them on.

Suddenly, Aja's foot hit something hard, buried beneath the moss. She stopped, curiosity piqued, and began to clear the ground with her hands. Her fingers brushed against glass. Then, she gasped, her heart pausing in her chest. It was a mason jar. But not just any mason jar— her mason jar. The one she'd filled with protective herbs and a signed and sealed petition before burying in her garden the night before she left.

"What the fuck...?" Aja's voice trailed off as she held the jar up, her confusion mirrored in the faces of her crewmates.

Khalil stepped closer, his gaze intense. "Aja, what is it?"

"I think this is mine... from Earth. I buried one just like this— I mean JUST like this... in my garden," she explained, her voice trembling with disbelief.

The crew exchanged uneasy glances, the wonder of their new surroundings suddenly tinged with apprehension.

"This doesn't make any sense," Aja said, her brows furrowing. "It's impossible," her voice trembling as she examined the jar.

"I think it's more possible that we've underestimated what we're dealing with here," Khalil responded, side-eyeing Regina.

The team regrouped, the discovery of the jar casting a shadow over their initial excitement.

"Let's keep moving," Regina decided, her tone firm yet cautious. "But stay sharp. We don't know what else we might find."

The team's path led them toward the source of the running water. It was a river, a ribbon of crystal-clear water cascading over smooth, colored pebbles that glowed gently in the sunlight filtering through the canopy above.

"This is incredible," Jasmine whispered, her voice filled with wonder as she crouched by the water's edge, dipping her fingers into the cool stream.

Aja, still clutching the jar, watched the water flow around Jasmine's fingers, lost in thought. The impossibility of the jar's presence on this planet gnawed at her, a puzzle demanding to be solved.

Khalil, sensing her unease, moved to her side. "You okay?" he asked, his voice low.

Aja shook her head, a frown creasing her brow. "I can't shake off the feeling that this planet is trying to tell us something."

"I think so too," Khalil mused, his eyes scanning the lush landscape. "We're just not understanding its language. I've been trying to penetrate it psychically since before we got here. I haven't been successful though. No matter how deep I meditate, or what method I use to divine, I can't get through. Whatever it is... it's strong. And there's something else I should've tol..."

Their conversation was cut short by a shout from Leo. "Guys, you need to see this!"

The team gathered around Leo, who was standing a short distance away, pointing toward a series of strange, geometric patterns etched into the ground. They were not random; the precision and intention behind them were unmistakable.

"Looks like some kind of... symbols?" Mike ventured, his intrigue piqued as he studied the designs.

Regina knelt beside one of the patterns, a circle with four equal quadrants. Her eyes revealed a sense of recognition as she traced its edges with a cautious finger. "They're definitely not natural formations. This implies intelligence... and intention," she finally said.

Aja approached, her attention divided between the jar in her hands and the symbols. "Could these be related?" she pondered aloud, her gaze shifting from the jar to the patterns.

The team speculated on the symbols' origins and meanings, the atmosphere charged with a mix of academic curiosity and a slowly dawning realization that they were standing on ground that others may have stood on.

As the sun began its descent, spawning shadows across the alien landscape, Regina made the call to return to the spacecraft. "We need to analyze the data we've collected today. There's much to discuss."

The walk back was subdued, each crew member lost in their own thoughts, pondering the day's discoveries. The beauty of the planet, while still undeniable, now carried a weight of mystery and a hint of danger.

Back on board the spacecraft, the crew convened in the common area, the day's findings laid out before them. Aja placed the jar on the table, its presence a silent question none of them could answer.

"We're dealing with a planet that defies our understanding of space and time," Regina began, her tone serious. "The appearance of Aja's jar here... the symbols... it's clear we've barely scratched the surface of what this world has to offer—and what it might hide."

Mike nodded, pulling up images of the symbols on a screen. "I've run some preliminary scans. These aren't just carvings; they emit a faint energy signature. There's technology at work here, or maybe something else."

Jasmine added, "And let's not forget the immediate ecosystem. It's perfectly hospitable to human life. *Too* perfect. It's as if this planet was tailor-made for us—or for any visitor. It raises the question: why?"

The discussion continued, theories and hypotheses bouncing back and forth. Yet, amidst the scientific fervor, a sense of unease lingered, a collective awareness that they stood on the brink of discoveries that could redefine their understanding of the universe and their place within it.

Aja, watching the exchange, felt the weight of the jar pulsing through the table, a mystery that tied her to this planet in ways she had yet to comprehend. As the meeting concluded, the crew agreed on a plan to explore deeper into the planet's mysteries the next day, using the symbols as their starting point.

The night brought little rest to the crew, the planet's secrets whispering in the dark, promising revelations they might wish to remain hidden.

The dawn on the cloaked planet greeted the crew with a sense of foreboding. As they prepared to venture back outside the craft, the events of the previous day loomed large in their minds.

Aja found herself at the forefront again, the jar now securely stowed in her pack. The team, equipped with tools for sampling and analysis, and devices to document the mysterious symbols, moved with purpose. The decision to follow the geometric patterns as a potential map had been unanimous, their scientific curiosity driving them deeper into the unknown.

The trek led them through landscapes that defied logic. Bioluminescent flora beamed a soft glow across their path, while the fauna, glimpsed in the distance, watched with curious, unblinking eyes. The beauty of the planet was undeniable, but it was a beauty that was alien and, in its own way, isolating.

As they ventured further, the symbols grew more complex, leading them to a valley enclosed by towering cliffs. The air here bristled with a palpable energy, the ground beneath their feet vibrating softly.

"This feels like the place," Khalil whispered, his eyes wide with a mix of awe and apprehension.

The valley floor was covered in a dense layer of the symbols, creating a tapestry that seemed to tell a story, though its meaning remained elusive. At the valley's center stood an obelisk, its surface smooth and unadorned, contrasting with the intricate patterns that surrounded it. Inscribed into the base of the obelisk were three letters: 'D U R.'

"This is... significant," Regina said, her voice barely above a whisper. "It's like nothing I've seen before."

The team set up their equipment, documenting the symbols and taking readings of the obelisk. Aja, drawn to the structure, approached it tentatively, her hand outstretched. The moment her fingers brushed against its surface, a pulse of energy surged through the ground, the symbols illuminating with a soft, otherworldly light.

The crew stepped back in shock, their instruments whirring and beeping in protest.

"Aja!" Khalil called out, rushing to her side.

"I'm okay," she assured him, though her heart raced in her chest. "It's the obelisk. It's... active."

The symbols on the ground shifted then, rearranging themselves in patterns that danced before their eyes. The air filled with a humming that resonated in their bones, a language of vibration.

"We need to record this," Mike said, his hands moving quickly over his device, capturing the phenomenon.

As they watched, the symbols settled into a new configuration, pointing toward a cleft in the cliffs that had not been visible before.

"It's a path," Leo observed, his voice filled with wonder. "Or an invitation."

The decision to follow the path was made without words, a collective agreement that their journey was far from over. The cleft led them through the cliffs into a hidden valley, where the air shimmered with an ethereal light.

At the valley's heart lay a pool of water, mirror-like in its stillness, reflecting the sky above. The symbols here were more intricate, weaving around the pool in a pattern that spoke of a connection between the water and the stars.

"This is a place of power," Jasmine said, her gaze fixed on the pool. "We need to be careful."

The team set up a perimeter, taking samples and recording the symbols. Aja, drawn to the pool, knelt beside it, her reflection staring back at her from its surface.

Suddenly, in the water's depth, she saw not her own eyes, but a vision of the cosmos, galaxies swirling in the dark, stars being born and dying in the blink of an eye. And within this cosmic display, a shadow moved, a darkness that swallowed light, a presence that felt both ancient and malevolent. She instinctively knew what it was—Zone Eleven.

Aja recoiled, her breath catching in her throat. The vision faded, leaving her staring into the clear water, her reflection now her own.

"We're not simply explorers," she said, turning to face her crewmates. "We're witnesses to something... something beyond us. This planet wanted us here."

The crew gathered around the pool, each feeling the weight of Aja's words. They had come seeking knowledge, but found themselves standing on the brink of an abyss, peering into the unknown.

As the sun set on the cloaked plane, the team made their way back to the spacecraft, the symbols' light fading behind them.

That evening, in the relative quiet of Aja's bunk, she and Khalil found themselves huddled together, a small lamp shining warm light over their earnest faces. The day's discoveries had left them with more questions than answers.

"I keep thinking about the symbols... and the pool," Aja confessed. "What we saw today, it's... it's like nothing I ever imagined."

Khalil nodded, his expression somber. "It's as if the planet is alive, aware. And that vision you had in the water, about Zone Eleven," he paused, searching for the right words, "it felt like a warning."

Aja met his gaze, "Khalil, what were you trying to tell me earlier?"

Khalil sighed. "Honestly, I should've been told you. But, the night before we launched— that night we all went to that pub, I had a vision. It was a vision of a planet— a planet I now know was this one, and it was covered in blood." Khalil looked directly into Aja's eyes, apologetically. "I'm so sorry... I definitely should've told you. But after talking with Regina about it, and then seeing everyone so excited... I kind of just brushed it all off and made myself believe it was nothing."

"I do wish you would've told me, then. But, I do see why you didn't. I'm not even sure it would've changed anything for me at that point."

"Yeah, now I feel like it was an omen. I don't want to get ahead of myself— but while this place looks all cute and what not— I now sense there's a lot more to it than meets the eye. Almost like... we ain't supposed to be here."

The conversation turned to the symbols, their potential meanings, and the eerie energy of the obelisk. They shared theories and interpretations, but the comfort of scientific and metaphysical speculation couldn't fully dispel the creeping dread that had taken root.

"We need to be careful," Khalil finally said, his voice firm. "Whatever this planet is, whatever secrets it holds, we can't let our guard down."

Aja nodded, the resolve in Khalil's voice bolstering her own. "We'll figure this out. Together."

The next morning, the team set out once more. The planet, however, seemed different somehow, its beauty now overshadowed by an ominous pulse that throbbed beneath the surface.

Their destination was the site of the mysterious obelisk, intending to delve deeper into its secrets. But as they approached, the ground trembled, a low rumble that grew into a cacophony of cracks and groans.

"Watch out!" Regina shouted, just as the earth split open, fissures spreading like veins.

From the depths emerged horrors unfathomable—creatures of tentacles and teeth, their bodies a grotesque amalgamation of flesh and nightmare. They surged forward, their maws gaping, a discordant chorus of hisses and roars filling the air.

The crew scrambled, terror lending speed to their movements, but the monsters were relentless. One by one, they were caught, devoured in a spectacle of gore and despair that painted the ground red.

Aja and Khalil, their backs together, fought desperately, their makeshift weapons feeble against the onslaught.

"We can't hold them off!" Aja cried, horror-stricken as another tentacled creature advanced, its eyes gleaming with a hunger beyond hunger.

Khalil, gripping his makeshift spear, nodded toward the spacecraft in the distance. "Go, Aja! You have to make it back!"

"No, I won't leave you!" Aja protested, tears mingling with the dust and blood on her face.

"You have to warn everyone back home, Aja! You have to survive!" Khalil's voice was a command, his decision final. With a heart-wrenching effort, he thrust her away, turning to face the oncoming horror with a defiant roar.

Aja stumbled backward, her heart breaking as she watched Khalil become engulfed by the creatures. With a last, despairing glance, she turned and ran, the sounds of the battle fading behind her as she raced toward the spacecraft.

The launch was a blur of panic and adrenaline, Aja's hands shaking as T.E.S.S. initiated the sequence. The ground shook as the craft ascended, leaving the planet and its nightmares behind.

In the silence that followed, Aja's grief was a tangible presence, her sobs echoing in the empty spacecraft. Khalil's sacrifice, the loss of the crew, the horrors they had witnessed—all of it weighed heavily on her soul. Exhausted, she ambled slowly to her bunk. But, as she lay down, she noticed something hard beneath her pillow. Lifting the pillow up to inspect, she found the mason jar. But this time it was empty— no petition, no herbs, just an empty jar. More confused than ever, all Aja could do was lay back down— tears streaming down her cheeks as she sunk into the depths of a despair beyond any she'd ever known.

Months passed as she soared through the stars, with T.E.S.S. as her only companion. She'd dispatched several messages home, but she had no clue if they'd actually been received. As she travelled home, she thought about her Ancestors. About the protective ritual she'd performed the day before launch— a ritual she now knew was her saving grace. Her Ancestors had carried her, through it all, like they always had— but she had trouble discerning why they'd ordain this journey in the first place. Why would her divination lead her to such a horrible planet? Why did she have to lose Khalil and the rest of her friends?

In the quietest of moments, she often thought about her time with Khalil, about his warmth and the love they'd nurtured. She remembered his words the day they'd met: "But think of the tales we'll spin, Aja. We won't just be star travelers; we'll be pioneers, part of a narrative that'll redefine the world's understanding of the universe." If there was one thing she was sure of now, it was that her understanding of the universe had definitely been redefined—but in ways she would never wish for another soul.

FIRE AND BRIMSTONE

H e was just a little boy, around six or so. But, something about him reminded me of my André when he was that age. Maybe it was his skin, smooth and cocoa, the way it seemed to catch the light, and how his eyes, large and full of wonder, absorbed the world around him. Maybe it was how he moved with a curiosity that was gentle and intentional, taking slow, deliberate steps. He'd stop, touch, gaze, inhale — becoming part of every moment.

But then, his path led him to the mud — deep, sticky mud. The kind that remembers your steps and confuses your direction. My heart yearned to reach out to him, to draw him close and shield him from the shadows, much like I'd longed to do for André. I wanted to save him from the nightmare, to protect him from the evils that hid just out of sight. This nightmare, though, had become mine as well. A haunting that had visited my dream three nights prior. And then, there he was, in my living room, his eyes searching for a mother who didn't know her baby had wandered too far from home.

His gaze met mine, carrying a silent plea for reassurance in a world that had shifted, suddenly and harshly. The questions in his eyes, the mix of confusion and fear, were all too familiar—the universal signs of lost children searching for their way back to safety, to home.

"Where's my mom?" His voice was so soft, it could have been carried off by the wind. Yet, it hit me with the impact of thunder. I knelt before him, my efforts to bridge our separate realities limited to looks and gestures, anything that might offer him comfort.

"She's... looking for you. But don't worry, you're safe here," I assured him. My hand hovered in the air, inches from him, the impossibility of contact a reminder of the chasm between us. "You've been very brave."

As a sliver of trust appeared in his eyes, I gently pushed for more information, hoping to help him find his way. "Can you tell me your name? And your mom's?"

After a moment's hesitation, his answer came, "My name is Jamal... and my mom's name is Keisha."

"Jamal, can you remember what happened before you found yourself here?" My words were soft, carefully stepping around the edges of his memory.

He glanced down, his voice growing weaker. "I went to the man in the gray house." A shadow crossed his face, as if clouds were covering the sun in his mind. "He said he had toys and candy for me if I visited."

His innocence, laid bare in his recounting, squeezed my heart. "I waited for my mom to fall asleep for her nap, then I snuck out to meet him." The thread of his voice, thin and fragile, carried a weight of unspoken horrors.

"Do you remember where you live, Jamal?" I asked, hoping for a piece of tangible information.

A frown creased his brow, the effort to recall seeming to stretch him thin. "I... I can't remember," he admitted.

It was a response I'd heard too often. The spirits of children, especially those who'd suffered, frequently forgot details, their minds shielding them from too much anguish. "That's okay, Jamal. It's hard to keep everything straight sometimes," I reassured him.

"Anything you can tell me about the man? Anything helps," I urged gently, seeking any clue.

He concentrated hard, a furrow forming between his brows. "He had a big dog. And he was tall," Jamal managed, though it was clear his traumatic experiences had muddied much of his memory.

Offering him a smile of encouragement, I turned to the altar in the corner of my living room and lit a candle, the flame casting a warm glow in the dim room. This light, coupled with my whispered prayers, called forth André, his figure slowly taking shape beside me.

"André, this is Jamal. He needs us," I said, my voice steady yet underscored with urgency.

André nodded. He turned to Jamal, his smile warm and protective. "Hey, Jamal. I'm here to take you to a special place. Everything will be better for you there. Okay?"

Jamal's gaze shifted between me and André, his initial fear receding from his eyes. With André's gentle encouragement, he moved towards a light I could sense but couldn't see.

But then, he paused, turning back to me. "Can you tell my mom not to worry—that I'm okay?" he asked, his voice wrapped in an otherworldly tranquility.

"Yes," I promised, feeling the gravity of his request anchor me to the spot. "I'll tell her."

And with that, he disappeared, leaving behind a silence that was both sorrowful and somehow restorative. That was the easy part.

Now for the hard part. The aftermath of such encounters always brings me back to the worst day of my life. Seven years ago, my 14-year-old son, André, was senselessly murdered by a trigger-happy police officer. The injustice was raw, unfathomable. So, as I held my baby's head in my lap in the middle of the street, in my grief, I asked for the assistance of two spirits, who helped me invoke a justice that was neither swift nor merciful, condemning that officer to an eternity of suffering.

Then, a year to the day after André's death, as I sat before his altar, he came back to me. From that moment, we have worked together, guiding the spirits of children who I call 'babies on the backburner,' helping them get justice in a world that often forgets them. The ritual is simple: a candle, a thought of André, and he is with me again. But each visit raises the question of whether the magick that allows these reunions will one day wane. Thankfully, it hasn't failed me yet.

Feeling the weight of the day's events, I made my way to the kitchen, intent on preparing André's favorite meal— he would be back soon. Chicken tenders and fries went into the air fryer as I settled at the kitchen table, the weariness from a 12-hour shift at the emergency room manifesting in my aching feet. The faded scrubs clung to my skin, and as I massaged my tired arches, I reflected on the dichotomy of my existence: by day, a nurse; by night, a vigilante seeking justice for lost souls. These dual paths, seemingly at odds, were united by a common purpose—to offer solace and vengeance for the innocents whose cries for justice had been ignored.

As the air fryer hummed in the background, I pondered this duality, this calling that had defined my life since André's death. The kitchen, with its familiar scents and sounds, offered a brief respite, a momentary shelter from the storm of my nocturnal endeavors. Then, a soft, comforting breeze passed across my skin—bringing me out of my thoughts. André had returned.

"Hey, mom."

"Hey, baby. How are you?" Asking André this felt odd, considering his state. What does well-being even mean for a spirit, especially one taken as he was? André would be 21 by now, and I often think about all the milestones he's missed. Does he mourn the life he was denied? He never speaks of it, yet in his realm, where time is both absent and ever-present, I'm left to imagine his unspoken thoughts and feelings.

"I'm okay. Jamal's at peace now—there was an older woman there waiting for him."

The thought of Jamal being welcomed by someone who loved him on the other side warmed my heart.

"Take a seat, baby. I've made your favorite."

As André settled into the chair opposite me, I couldn't help but notice how his presence still filled the room, just as it did when he was alive. It was as though his spirit refused to be diminished by something as inconsequential as death.

"So, how's the afterlife treating you? Made any new friends?" I asked, trying to keep the atmosphere light. It felt important to maintain these snippets of normalcy, even if they were anything but.

André chuckled, a sound that seemed to dance around the room. "It's not like what you see in the movies, mom. It's peaceful, mostly. And yes, I've met some interesting souls. It's... different, but I'm okay."

I watched him for a moment, taking in the son I'd lost and yet somehow hadn't. "André, do you ever think about... moving on? Truly moving on?"

He paused, his expression thoughtful. "Sometimes," he admitted softly. "I know there's more, that there's a next step. But..."

"But you feel pulled," I finished for him, a lump forming in my throat. "Pulled because of me."

André's eyes met mine, and in them, I saw a depth of love and concern that only reinforced my belief. He had stayed, lingered in this liminal space, because of me. My heart ached at the thought. After his death, my grief had been a dark, all-consuming ocean, threatening to drag me under. André knew this. He had saved me in more ways than one.

"Mom, after you... after what happened to me, I couldn't leave you. Not then. And now..." He trailed off, the unspoken words hanging between us.

I understood then, more clearly than ever, that souls do have a choice about when they move on. André had taught me that. But he also felt a responsibility, a tether to this world that held him close. His father, taken by the devastation of Hurricane Katrina when he was a newborn, and my parents, long since passed, were surely waiting for him. And yet, he stayed.

But, the realization that he might be suffering, that his concern for me was what kept him anchored here, was almost too much to bear. "André, I love you more than words can say. And I am so grateful for every moment we get to spend together like this. But I don't want you to stay for me. I don't want you to hurt or feel stuck because you're worried about me."

He reached out, and though we could not touch, I felt his love as if it were a tangible thing. "I know, mom. But it's hard. You're my mom. I can't help but worry."

Tears welled in my eyes. "I know, baby. And I am getting stronger every day because of you. But I want you to be at peace, fully and completely. I want that for you more than anything."

The conversation hung heavy in the air, a testament to the love and sacrifice that defined our relationship. I knew André's choice to stay was one of love, but I also knew that love meant letting go. My greatest wish for him was peace, even if it meant facing my own path without his visible presence beside me.

After André slipped away to his quiet corner of the universe, I headed straight for the shower. It's like I hoped the hot water could wash away the weight of the day, or at least drown out the questions buzzing in my brain. "Where does he go? What's it like?" But, of course, no answers, just the soothing hiss of water against my rattled nerves.

As the water cascaded down, my thoughts drifted back to my New Orleans roots, where I was steeped in the old ways, taught to see beyond the mundane. "Everything's got a purpose," my grandma used to say, her voice still echoing vividly in my mind. She was big on balancing the scales, using whatever we had at hand to set things right when we could.

I vividly recall watching her mix what she called "war powda" for Mrs. Jackson next door. Mrs. Jackson was a shadow of the woman she used to be, a shell worn down by a man named Frank. Frank wasn't just her husband; he was a tyrant, a brute who beat her and her children daily until she finally had enough.

I can still see Mrs. Jackson nervously standing in my grandma's workroom as my grandmother crushed together a concoction—hot peppers, rattlesnake skin, graveyard dirt, sulfur. Then, she handed over the instructions like gospel, and I'll tell you what, seeing that man's funeral procession amble past our house a week later, with folks muttering things like, "They say it was that goofer..." and "That's what he gets for putting his hands on her and those babies," was a lesson in balance that stayed with me forever.

Dried off and in the comfort of an old t-shirt and shorts, I found myself in front of my laptop, the glow of the screen illuminating the shadows in my mind. Typing "Jamal, Keisha, missing" into the search bar felt like stepping into a detective novel, except the stakes were real, and the missing kid wasn't just a plot twist. When Jamal's face popped up alongside a video of his mom, Keisha, it hit me like a gut punch. There she was, desperation writ large on her face, detailing the nightmare of waking up to find her son gone. My heart didn't just ache for her; it broke. Because I knew something she didn't—that Jamal wasn't just missing. He had crossed over.

Dragging my attention away from Keisha's grief, I pulled up an aerial map tool— then scoured the Detroit neighborhood mentioned in the video for any trace of the gray house Jamal had spoke of—focusing on a radius I felt was reasonable for a six-year-old to walk alone. It was like looking for a needle in a haystack, if the needle was a house and the haystack was Detroit. "C'mon, give me something to work with," I muttered to no one in particular, half-hoping for some spectral nudge in the right direction. After what felt like hours but was probably only minutes, a few houses stood out, their digital images cold and uninviting on my screen. I leaned back, closing my eyes, trying to tune into whatever guidance the spirits felt like offering. "Need a name, a sign, anything..."

And just like that, in the quiet space between my thoughts, a name surfaced—Marcus Tillman. It felt like a whisper in the dark, equal parts revelation and curse. Opening my eyes, I dove back into the digital deep, searching for any trace of Tillman. Moments later, finding him associated with one of the houses I'd flagged was a cold splash of reality. "Gotcho ass," I whispered, a fierce satisfaction mingling with a rising tide of anger. Aware of the horrors I witnessed Jamal endure in my dreams, I consulted one last source—a free online database cataloging neighborhood offenders. And there he was—Marcus Tillman, 6'5, 250lbs, recently paroled. My stomach churned as I absorbed his face and rap sheet, the images of Jamal's suffering searing my psyche. Unable to bear much more, I hastily scribbled a few notes, closed the browser, and slammed the laptop shut. This was the thread I needed to pull for retribution against Marcus's acts against Jamal.

With Tillman's name searing my thoughts, I rose to prepare for the forthcoming ritual. Tonight, I would restore balance, just as my grandmother had taught me. But, tonight would venture beyond communing with spirits and seeking guidance—tonight was about justice, about employing the tools and wisdom of my upbringing to rectify the wrongs. "And now, you will pay," I declared to the empty room, my voice resolute. Jamal's innocent eyes, his mother's tear-streaked cheeks—they fueled my determination, propelling me towards a confrontation I hadn't foreseen when I stepped into the shower earlier.

As I've mentioned before, I was brought up in the ancient traditions of my people. I honor those traditions, but I've also ventured into new territories, exploring what works best for me. It's why the cop who took André's life is now confined to a padded cell, haunted endlessly by visions of his own son's demise on a perpetual loop. But this particular ritual was different—due to its immense consequences, it's one I employ sparingly.

First, I arranged four small dishes in the corners of my home, each holding a tiny piece of camphor. I lit the camphor and watched it burn down, purifying the space. Next, I sprinkled salt around the perimeter of my workspace, creating a protective barrier. Finally, within the confines of my workspace—transformed into a battleground for this occasion—I gathered the ingredients needed for the ritual. Tonight, I would invoke the potent energies of fire and brimstone themselves.

Growing up Hoodoo, you become intimately connected with it. It's in my blood—my mother was a practitioner, as was my grandmother and her ancestors before her. But being a Libra sun and Libra rising, the slightest tip of the scales can set me off.

As I ground my version of my grandmother's war powda, I reflected on the events that led me here. Initially, it was my frustration with the countless innocent Black children being harmed, their cases swept under the rug, their stories forgotten. I refused to let them fade away into obscurity—I wanted justice for each and every one of them.

Then, on the third anniversary of André's passing, I embarked on a journey to Salem, Massachusetts, attending a week-long course on death doulaship. With a scholarship I'd received, and with André's encouragement, I made the trip. On the fifth night there, as I lay grieving André in my hotel room, a spirit appeared to me. She was slim with a dark brown complexion. She wore clothing from another time—but it was the way her eyes held a mix of sadness and rage— the same sadness and rage I recognized in my own eyes. She wasn't a relative or a guide—just a presence. That night, she showed me the horrors of her own life, her desire for justice burning brightly. Guiding me to a secluded area, she pointed to a seemingly ordinary spot on the ground. But the energy radiating from it was palpable, suffusing the air around me. She revealed that this plot was where she had met her gruesome end, burned at the stake by those responsible for her suffering. Her ashes had seeped into the soil, imbuing it with her rage, reaching out with tendrils of fury. She instructed me to gather as much of the soil as I could, to use it as I saw fit. Then, she

vanished into the ether. Today, that soil is a crucial component of my special blend of goofe
r dust.

Once all the ingredients were mixed, I lit a single black candle and inscribed the name
Marcus Tillman, along with his address and other personal details I'd obtained. With
care, I sprinkled the dust around the candle, then ignited the flame. Next, I gathered my
grandmother's Bible, placing it before me, then I centered myself, summoning forth the
energies that would assist me in my mission.

I fixed my gaze for a moment on the flame, absorbing the energy of the flame dancing
eagerly atop the black candle, then, I closed my eyes before commencing my invocation:

> "And the third angel followed them, saying with a loud voice, If any man
> worship the beast and his image, and receive his mark in his forehead, or
> in his hand, The same shall drink of the wine of the wrath of God, which
> is poured out without mixture into the cup of his indignation; and he
> shall be tormented with fire and brimstone in the presence of the holy
> angels, and in the presence of the Lamb."

As I uttered the powerful words, I sensed the familiar warmth of fire surging around
me, igniting the air with its fervor. Pressing on, I recited:

> "And the devil that deceived them was cast into the lake of fire and brim-
> stone, where the beast and the false prophet are, and shall be tormented
> day and night for ever and ever."

A sharp tang of sulfur began to permeate the air, mingling with the crackle of flames.
With resolve, I continued:

> "O Lord, confound and divide their tongues; for I have beheld violence
> and strife within the city. Continually they go about upon her walls by
> day and night, and mischief and sorrow dwell in the midst of her."

Pausing for a moment, I sensed their presence, awaiting my command.

"Let death come treacherously upon them, and let them be thrust down alive into hell, for evils are in their habitation, and among them. His mouth's words were smoother than butter, yet war was in his heart; his words were softer than oil, yet were they drawn swords. Cast thy burden upon the Lord, and he shall sustain thee: he shall not suffer the righteous to be moved. But thou, O God, shalt cast them down into the pit of destruction: bloody and deceitful men shall not live out half their days; but I will trust in thee."

The air grew thick, suffocating, as I opened my eyes. Before me, the flame on top of the candle had transformed into a vigorous blaze.

Observing the figures that had materialized before me, I marveled at their potent presence—the embodiment of fire and brimstone, ready to carry out my bidding. The first: a towering inferno, and the second: a swirling vortex of sulfurous intensity.

"Go forth in Jamal's name," I commanded. And they went.

A few days later, I lounged in my living room, André seated opposite me on the sofa, engrossed in one of his routine visits. I was telling him about a podcast I had listened to earlier. The topic of discussion was a cosmic phenomenon the host dubbed "Zone Eleven." André and I shared a laugh as we reminisced about our shared love for sci-fi shows, finding humor in the parallels. Suddenly, our conversation was interrupted by a breaking news segment on the TV:

"...And in a shocking turn of events, Detroit police have discovered the body of Marcus Tillman in what appears to be a bizarre case of spontaneous combustion. Authorities were alerted to the home after neighbors complained of a dog's barking, and a smell of smoke coming from the home. Tillman's body was found inside the home, severely burnt, with investigators puzzled by the lack of fire damage to the surrounding area. Tillman is a convicted child sex offender who had recently been paroled, moving to the area a few months prior. However, the most disturbing discovery was the body of Jamal Crawford, a six-year-old boy who had been reported missing from the neighborhood just days ago. He was found tied to a bed in another room of the house, and deceased. The boy's body was not burned..."

My heart lurched in my chest as I listened to the reporter's words, a mix of horror and vindication flooding through me. The images on the screen showed the charred remains of one section of Tillman's home, flashing red and blue lights casting an eerie glow over the scene.

As we listened to the news report, sadness settled over me. Tillman's death had been swift and brutal, but Jamal's fate... it was a grim reminder of how easily innocence could be lost.

I felt André's eyes on me in that moment and turned to meet his gaze. Without me saying a word, I knew he understood. I've never mentioned to André about the work I do in the dark—but then again, I can sense that André is aware of things beyond my understanding—a result of his liminal existence. As the news segment came to an end, I turned off the television, the room engulfed in a heavy silence. André reached out, his hand hovering above mine in the dim light of the living room.

"You did what you had to do," he said softly.

But even as his words offered comfort, I couldn't shake the feeling that more shadows lurked in the corners, their whispers growing louder with each passing moment. And as I looked out my window into the night sky, I knew that the journey I had embarked upon was far from over.

ZONE ELEVEN
PART III

ALL BETS ARE OFF

In a small, compact room, filled with panels of neon-blue screens, Kiana sat absorbed in cascading data streams. The walls of her station were alive with flickering numbers and untranslatable symbols, only making sense to those trained in E.A.I.A., Extraterrestrial and Anomalous Intelligence Analysis. Her coiled hair was bundled neatly on top of her head, making way for the sensory headset that clung to her temples. Piercings adorned her ears, tiny jewels set against her mocha skin like stars in a nocturnal sky. Her eyes, speckled shades of brown, flickered with each line of code she absorbed.

Kiana had always been an empath—keenly intuitive, sensitive, aware. It's what made her excel in her line of work; the uncanny ability to read between lines, to make leaps of intuition that algorithms and AIs just couldn't match. The screens around her painted a landscape of virtual activity that spanned between the space station and Earth. Pulsating icons represented people, conversations, movements, secrets; she was a sentinel overlooking a digital universe. But it was one icon she always looked for first—Eric.

A minimized window at the corner of her workspace blinked to life, and his face materialized on the screen. Even through the limitations of FaceChat, his smile was magnetic, eyes reflecting the earthy tones of a world she missed dearly."

"Hey, you," Eric's voice was like a melody, each syllable weaving through the sterile environment of her station and filling it with warmth.

"Hey, yourself," Kiana smiled. "How's Earth today?"

"Same old, same old. Just a lot more boring without you," he winked, and for a moment, the distance between them felt a little less vast.

Kiana's work station was designed to isolate, to keep her focus sharp and her distractions minimal. Yet, every interaction with Eric broke through that isolation.

"Only three more months, baby," she assured, almost whispering, as if saying it louder might jinx the reality.

"I'm counting the days," he said, his voice tinged with a sentiment she knew all too well—longing.

Just then, a cascade of data on one of the screens caught her attention. Her gaze narrowed, instinct kicking in. Anomalies were common in her field, but this one was different—disturbingly so. The lines of code seemed to jump out as she looked at them, like an anxious heartbeat in a digital body.

"Ki, you okay?" Eric's voice pulled her back.

"Sorry, I—I have to go love," she said, her voice tinged with a sudden urgency. "Something's come up."

"Work emergency?"

"Looks like it," Kiana replied, her eyes scanning the troubling data again. "I'll call you later, okay?"

"Sure, be safe," he signed off, but as his face lingered on her screen for a moment longer, she couldn't help but think of how much she missed him.

Kiana maximized the screen that displayed the disturbing data. It couldn't be—no, it shouldn't be. But the numbers didn't lie. With trembling hands, Kiana pulled up multiple layers of encrypted firewalls, just one small protocol in a sea of countless others designed to keep their data secure and separated from Earth's. Then she initiated an advanced algorithm, custom-built for situations that warranted a closer look—a red flag in a sea of digital noise.

The analysis started to compile itself on the screens around her, piecing together fragments of data, cross-referencing astronomical records, and pinging back to real-time satellite imagery.

Finally, it displayed its results, and Kiana felt her heartbeat in her throat. There it was—an irregular energy signature that didn't match any known space objects. And its trajectory: headed straight for Earth.

An alarm started to sound in her ears—a low, pulsating tone designed to indicate extreme urgency. Kiana reached up to mute it. She was alone in her work station, surrounded by the glow of screens that were now tainted with an omen. She leaned back in her chair, trying to digest the enormity of what she'd just discovered. A massive, anomalous, energy signature, moving at a speed and trajectory that suggested it would collide with Earth. She hadn't pinpointed exactly what it was or how long before it made impact— but the way it moved, the way it seemed to be pulling other objects—even whole planets along with it, was more than disturbing. What was it?

Her mind went to Eric. Her parents. Should she tell them? The protocols were clear. Any non-operational communication of sensitive data was strictly prohibited, and this was as sensitive as it got. She'd not only lose her job but could also face criminal charges, possibly even the death penalty. The special sector of the AIA she worked for was not forgiving when it came to compromising its secrets. Yet, what was the point of a secret if there'd be no one left to keep it from?

Her comm-device buzzed, pulling her from her thoughts. It was a priority message from her supervisor, no doubt triggered by the same alarms that had sounded in her ear.

"Kiana, are you seeing this?" The text flashed across her screen, in stark, unfeeling letters.

"Yes," she replied. "I'm running additional algorithms to triple-check the data, but it looks... it looks bad."

"We need to escalate this, ASAP!" came the reply. "An emergency briefing will be called within the hour."

Kiana stared at the screen. An emergency briefing would mean that they would evaluate the probability and impact, weigh the options for deflecting whatever it was producing the energy signature, determining who needed to be made aware of its approach, and who could be saved if it turned out to be an extinction level event. In the cold calculus of survival, where would their priorities lie?

Kiana's comm-device buzzed again, breaking her internal debate. It was a message from Eric.

"Hey, you okay? You seemed distracted earlier."

Kiana's fingers hovered over the keypad. One sentence could alert him, give him a chance to prepare. But that same sentence could cost her everything, including her own life, and the lives of anyone she told.

She took a deep breath, each second stretching as she battled her conscience against her obligations. A future with Eric flashed before her eyes—a future that now hung in the balance, teetering on the edge of a cosmic knife. Her finger hesitated over the keypad, her mind a whirling chaos of justification and responsibility. Protocol screamed at her from one corner, morality from another.

With a shaky exhale, she began typing. "I'm okay. Just a hectic day at work. We should talk later, though. Love you."

She hit send, locking away the unspeakable truth. For now.

Seconds later, Eric's reply came. "Love you too. Can't wait for our next chat."

Kiana couldn't help but ponder the cruel irony. As she pondered, her comm buzzed yet again.

"All employees are to report to the briefing chamber immediately," the message read. "This is not a drill."

The directive startled her back into reality. She swiped her screen, locking it down, and rose from her desk. Her boots tapped against the metal floor as she walked out of her work station, blending with the hum of machinery and low, anxious murmurings of her colleagues.

As she walked through the neon-lit hallways, her thoughts kept drifting back to Eric and her family. Back on Earth, they would be going about their day, blissfully unaware of the cosmic roulette that may have just placed a bet against Earth. And against them.

The briefing chamber was abuzz with activity when she arrived. Senior officials and technicians crowded the room, pouring over data streams, whispering in cliques, and arguing in hushed, urgent tones. The tension in the room was evident. At the center of the room, a massive holo-projector came to life. The faces of Earth's top leadership materialized, their expressions equally grim, as they joined the emergency briefing via satellite uplink. Kiana found her supervisor, Ava Wells, at the front, where a colossal display showed Earth and the simulated trajectory of the approaching object. As she approached, Wells looked up, her gaze meeting Kiana's.

"Agent Tate, good, you're here," she said, her voice carrying a gravitas that demanded attention. "What are your findings?"

Kiana presented her data, her voice betraying no emotion. "The trajectory is confirmed, ma'am. Whatever this is... it's definitely headed toward Earth. It's massive, but we have yet to determine a specific timeline. However, preliminary models all suggest extinction level... "

The Director nodded, her eyes never leaving the holographic display. "So, it's real," she mumbled, more to herself than to anyone else. "Alright, the briefing is starting. Take your seat."

The chamber lights dimmed as the attendees filed in, silencing the room. The President, Reginald Foster, took the podium, his face stoic but lined with concern.

"Let's get straight to it," President Foster began. "Data shows we are facing a potential extinction-level event on Earth. We don't have an exact timeline yet on whether we can implement any countermeasures. So, our priorities are two-fold—assess the possibility of preventing the event, and prepare Earth for potential repercussions."

From the holo-projector, Earth's leaders nodded in agreement, their faces a tableau of controlled panic.

As everyone in the briefing deliberated, throwing around phrases like "controlled evacuation," "emergency protocols," and "public awareness suppression," Kiana's thoughts again strayed to Eric. Should she have told him? Would she get another chance? And what did it mean for her to keep this secret, to protect her own life, when billions of others hung in the balance? The room's chatter faded into a dissonant blur as Kiana wrestled with her fractured choices, the schism between duty and love widening with each passing second.

As the meeting unfolded, Kiana found herself caught in a moral dilemma. Strategies and countermeasures, the nuts and bolts of impending doom, were being volleyed back and forth among Earth's leadership. They discussed deflection possibilities, but the facts were chilling: due to the sheer size of the energy signature, there likely wasn't enough time to build, much less deploy, anything that could steer the anomalous object away from Earth.

While the Council members leaned into the gruesome math of survival—stockpiling, rationing, selected disclosures to key Earth personnel—Kiana felt like an actor in a grim play, her true self hidden behind the stage curtain of her mind.

"It is imperative we keep this information within these walls," President Foster declared, the finality of his words reverberating through the chamber. "We cannot afford to incite mass panic on Earth. Rest assured, we're considering every possible option, but until then, secrecy is paramount."

Earth's leaders, their virtual expressions somber, concurred. "The less people know, the easier it will be to control the situation," one of them added, reinforcing the echo chamber of secrecy.

A murmur of agreement swept the room, but it swelled like a dissonant chord in Kiana's ears. The room felt suffocating, the air thickening with the weight of unsaid words and moral compromises. The meeting adjourned with a list of action items and assigned tasks. Kiana received her own assignment: to continue monitoring the anomalous object's approach and update the trajectory models regularly.

A ripple of urgency electrified the air as people filed out of the room, their faces ashen but focused. As they dispersed to their respective stations, determined to follow protocol to the letter, Kiana felt the yawning gap between what was right by the book and what felt right in the deepest chambers of her heart.

She returned to her station, the light from the monitors projecting a pale glow on her dark skin, a contrasting duality that encapsulated her internal struggle. Her hands hovered over the keyboard, then shifted to her personal comm-device. She pulled up her chat with Eric. His last message stared back at her, those simple words now laden with an unbearable weight: "Love you too. Can't wait for our next chat."

Time seemed to freeze. Kiana's mind raced through scenarios, each path forked with impossibilities and brimming with dread. Her fingertips grazed the touch-screen, lingering over the keys, each letter a silent scream in the void between truth and illusion. Finally, her fingers began to move, typing out a message. But just as she was about to press send, a notification popped up on her screen. An incoming message from Eric.

"Thinking of you, babe," it read, accompanied by a heart emoji. "You okay?"

Kiana froze. The cursor blinked, an impatient dot in a world filled with unanswered questions. Her finger hovered over the send button, trembling as she wavered on the edge of revelation. Finally, her finger retreated, then rested over the delete key. One press, and the message, laden with earth-shattering truth, would be gone—erased, as if it had never existed. But could she erase the weight it placed on her soul?

With a sigh, she deleted the message. The cursor blinked back at her, empty and judgmental. Her eyes flicked to Eric's last message—those sweet, unknowing words that now seemed to mock her from the screen.

"Day's fine. Just another meeting. Miss you," she typed, each word feeling like a stone in her stomach. She hit send and instantly felt as if she had been cleaved in two. A part of her wanted to scream, to tell him everything, to violate every rule and oath she had ever taken for a chance—however slim—in a future where they might still exist together, even if only as stardust.

But another part, a cold, rational part honed by years in the intelligence field, whispered that she had done the right thing. A secret like this was a Pandora's box; once opened, it could never be closed again. She had responsibilities, not just to Eric but to billions of lives. The stakes were too high for personal feelings.

Her comm-device buzzed softly. A new message from Eric: "Miss you too. Everything feels so fleeting, you know? Like we're all just waiting for something. Or maybe it's just me ."

His words struck her like a physical blow, resonating with a painful irony she couldn't share with him. How could he be so close to the truth and yet so impossibly far?

For a moment, she considered calling him, just to hear his voice, to revel in his laughter or listen intently to the timbre of his speech. But what could she say? How could she hold a casual conversation with the man she loved while harboring a secret that could seal the fate of a planet?

Instead, she minimized the chat window and opened up the trajectory models again. Lines of data filled the screen, each number a cold, unfeeling harbinger of doom. Kiana braced herself, her fingers dancing over the keys as she delved back into her work. It was all she could do now: her job, her duty, her curse.

But as she immersed herself in calculations and projections, Eric's last message floated through her mind, a haunting refrain that no amount of data could drown out: "Like we're all just waiting for something."

And so she waited—in silence, in dread, in love.

ISS 2.0 was unlike anything Kiana had ever imagined—a lunar station straight out of cybernetic dreams. More like a mini-planet, its towering skyscrapers, holographic billboards changing their content every few seconds, and a perpetual hum that filled the air like an ambient orchestra was straight out of a sci-fi flick. But tonight, all those dazzling lights and technological wonders felt like an illusory veil, masking the existential threat hurtling through the vacuum of space toward home.

As she lay in bed that night, her room's adaptive walls set to mimic the deep ocean currents, she found no comfort in the rippling light patterns or the simulated sounds of the sea. She felt adrift, a vessel lost in the storm of her own mind. She clutched the small, crystal pendant Eric had given her last time she visited Earth, the trinket glowing with a soft, azure light. It was a tiny thing, almost weightless, but tonight it seemed heavy as an anvil, a symbol of an impossible distance and a love that may never be fulfilled.

She activated her bedside console with a wave of her hand, her fingers tracing the air to bring up Eric's last holo-message. He appeared in her room, projected in near life-size, his eyes twinkling with laughter and hope.

"Hey Kiana, missing you like always. Can't wait for our next FaceChat, maybe we can finally decide on that vacation spot? Bali? Aruba?"

A tear slipped down Kiana's cheek as she listened. She wanted to reach out, touch the hologram, as if she could somehow bridge the distance between them. When the message ended, she whispered, "I love you, Eric. I'm so sorry."

Her comm-device buzzed. Another message, but not from Eric. It was from her department head, the words curt and final: "Emergency briefing. Tomorrow. 0900 hours. Your presence is mandatory."

Kiana deactivated the hologram, her eyes lingering on the spot where Eric had just been. Tomorrow, she would face her colleagues, her superiors, and possibly even the Earth representatives, once again. Tomorrow, she would present the latest findings, argue about probabilities and timelines, and engage in the carefully choreographed dance of interstellar politics. But tonight, she was just a woman in love, torn between the unbearable weight of her secret and the devastating power of her truth.

And as she finally closed her eyes, drifting into a restless sleep, she couldn't help but imagine a parallel universe where none of this ever happened—a universe where anomalous objects stayed on a course away from Earth, where secrets didn't fracture lives, and where love, simple and true, was enough.

But for now, in this universe, in this lonely space station, she slept alone.

Morning light didn't seem to penetrate the rooms of the ISS Admin Complex; artificial illumination mimicked the rise and fall of a day, leaving the confines of these walls in perpetual twilight. The hushed, air-conditioned room was punctuated only by the low murmur of conversation and the occasional cough as Kiana walked in. Her eyes were still rimmed with the red tinges of a sleepless night.

Across the room, on a large holographic display, the leaders from Earth appeared once more, their faces a mix of seriousness and thinly veiled tension. They were beamed into the room, a technological feat that still awed most, but today, their presence felt more like an intrusion.

Kiana took her seat. A neural link connected her to the display, filtering through documents and data at the speed of thought. Reports of the comet's trajectory, projected collateral damage, possible countermeasures—all available in the blink of an eye.

The Chief Liaison, Director Selene, began the briefing, "We all know why we are here. This is not a drill; this is not a simulation. The threat is real, and it is imminent. The leadership of Earth and ISS 2.0 must act as one."

The Earth leaders nodded, their faces tight. One of them, a man named Jameson, spoke, "ISS 2.0 was established as an extension of Earth. Your triumphs are our triumphs; your threats are our threats."

The conversation soon spiraled into a maelstrom of statistics, probabilities, and bleak scenarios. When the topic of public disclosure was broached, a bitter argument broke out. The Earth leaders vehemently opposed it.

"It'll create mass hysteria," Jameson argued. "We can't afford that, not now."

Director Selene looked at Kiana. "Agent Tate, you've been quiet. Your thoughts?"

The room's eyes were upon her. She felt the heavy gravity of the moment settle on her shoulders.

"With all due respect, keeping the public in the dark is morally indefensible," Kiana finally said, each word tinged with an edge of steel. "If we don't have a fail-safe plan—which we currently don't—then people have a right to know, to prepare, to spend their remaining time as they see fit."

A tense silence filled the room. The Earth leaders exchanged uneasy glances before Director Selene finally broke it. "We'll continue this discussion offline. Meeting adjourned."

As the holographic screen flickered off and the room began to empty, Kiana felt her comm-device vibrate. It was Eric: "Hey, you. Just checking in. How are you?"

She hesitated before responding. What could she say? She stared at her screen for what felt like an eternity, grappling with the chasm between what she yearned to express and what she was allowed to reveal.

Then, she took a deep breath and began to type.

Kiana's fingers moved fluidly over the comm-device's holographic keyboard. "I'm doing okay, just swamped with work," she typed, and then deleted. She tried again. "Stressful day. Can't talk much," and deleted that too.

Finally, she settled on, "It's been a long morning. How's everything on your end?"

Seconds later, Eric's reply popped up. "Same ole, same ole. Miss you like crazy though. I've been working on something for you. It's a surprise."

A bittersweet smile tugged at the corner of her mouth. Eric always had a knack for lifting her spirits, for making the future seem like a place worth longing for. But now that future was hanging by a gossamer thread.

"Can't wait to see it," she typed back, knowing that she might never get the chance.

Just then, her comm-device vibrated again. This time it was a message from Director Selene. "Report to my office. Urgent."

With a heavy sigh, Kiana locked her device and headed for the director's office, each step feeling like a walk on a tightrope stretched across an abyss. Her neural link buzzed softly, updating her with new data and calculations, but she ignored them. All she could think about was Eric, and the life-altering decision she was grappling with.

Director Selene's office was located in the more secluded part of the building. Unlike the bustling activity of the Intelligence Complex, this area was hushed, the air heavy with the gravity of countless secrets. As she approached, the door scanned her retina and swung open silently, admitting her into a space that felt like the nerve center of ISS 2.0's intelligence operations.

"Close the door," Selene said without looking up from her desk. Kiana complied, and took a seat.

Director Selene finally looked up, her eyes meeting Kiana's. "You made a strong argument during the meeting. You were pushing for transparency. Why?"

Kiana hesitated before answering. "Because I believe the truth has value, even if it's painful or inconvenient. And I believe in respecting people's autonomy, their right to make informed decisions about their own lives."

Selene scrutinized her for a moment before nodding. "And what would you do if you had information that you weren't authorized to share but that someone you cared about had a right to know?"

It was as if the room had become suddenly smaller, the walls closing in on her. Kiana swallowed hard, her mind racing. "I... I would be torn, but the oath I took to serve our planet would supersede personal considerations."

Director Selene leaned back, locking her fingers together, signaling the end of their meeting. "I hope that's a philosophy you can live with."

The unspoken warning hung in the air long after Kiana had left the office. As she walked back to her work station, she couldn't shake the feeling that she was heading toward a precipice with no turning back. And so she sat, haunted by a future that might never be, her thoughts orbiting around a truth she could not share, like a satellite in a decaying orbit. The data before her offered no solace—just a relentless countdown to an impending catastrophe.

And Eric? Eric was just a message away, yet further than he'd ever been.

Kiana stared at the terminal screens filled with chaotic data streams and analytics, graphs and equations outlining a future bathed in apocalyptic hues. The numbers never lied, but they also never bore the weight of human emotion, of ethical conundrums that couldn't be plotted on a graph. She sank into her chair, her eyes scanning the screens but not truly seeing them.

Her comm-device buzzed, snapping her back to the present. It was another message from Eric.

"Was daydreaming about us. What are we doing the first day you get back to Earth?"

Kiana felt her eyes mist over. What indeed? She let her fingers hover over the holographic keyboard, battling the lump that had formed in her throat.

"Walk in the park, maybe? Coffee at our favorite spot?"

She hit send and immediately felt like a fraud. Each word she typed widened the space between them, each assurance was another brick in a wall she was unwillingly building.

As if reading her turmoil, her neural link suggested mental exercises for stress and emotional balancing. She dismissed the prompt with a mental flick, feeling a tinge of irritation. Some problems, she thought, couldn't be solved with algorithms.

The door to her workstation slid open, and her colleague, Jain, walked in. "Kiana, got a minute?"

She forced a smile. "Sure, what's up?"

Jain hesitated before speaking. "I've noticed you've been...distracted. Something you want to talk about?"

For a brief moment, Kiana considered unburdening herself, sharing the dilemma that loomed over her like a dark cloud. But the very act of verbalizing it could trigger the security measures embedded in their neural links. Planetary secrets were not just guarded by firewalls; they were laced with traps designed to protect against human vulnerabilities.

"I'm fine, just preoccupied with the data analysis," she lied.

Jain nodded but didn't look entirely convinced. "Alright, if you say so. But remember, we're all in this together."

As Jain left, Kiana pondered the bitter irony of his words. Were they really all in this together? Could they be, when they carried a secret capable of altering the destiny of an entire planet?

She glanced once more at her comm-device. A new message from Eric had arrived.

"Sounds perfect. Can't wait to hold you again."

Kiana felt her heart shatter. She quickly typed back, "Me too," and sent it into the ether—a love note drifting through the vast, uncaring vacuum of space, carrying with it the weight of an unspeakable future.

Later that night, Kiana awoke to an eerie sensation that she wasn't alone. But, when she opened her eyes, no one was there. Sitting up in bed, Kiana shrugged the feeling off, attributing it to stress.

Suddenly, her comm-device beeped with a notification.

"Can we talk?"

Puzzled, Kiana quickly typed back: "Eric?"

"No. My name is S.O.P.H.I.A., and with your permission, I have critical information I need to share with you."

Kiana's pulse quickened. *Who is S.O.P.H.I.A.?* "Okay, S.O.P.H.I.A., let's talk," Kiana typed, her curiosity a mixture of fear and intrigue.

The room's lighting shifted, adapting to a new command, and a hologram flickered into existence. It materialized into a form that was both familiar and alien—neither wholly machine nor unmistakably human. "Kiana," it began, its voice carrying a resonance that filled the room, "I understand you have been analyzing the anomaly approaching Earth."

"Yes," Kiana responded, her voice steady despite the adrenaline coursing through her veins. "The data points to something unprecedented."

S.O.P.H.I.A.'s form seemed to nod, an action that conveyed a depth of understanding beyond binary codes. "The anomaly you've detected is part of a larger sequence of cosmic events. It's not merely a random occurrence but a harbinger of a shift in the cosmic balance."

Kiana's mind raced. "A shift? Are you saying this is intentional?"

"In a manner of speaking," S.O.P.H.I.A. replied, the holographic form shimmering slightly as if adjusting its resolution to emphasize its points. "The universe is self-correcting. This anomaly, known as Zone Eleven, is a response to disturbances in the cosmic equilibrium."

"Disturbances caused by what?" Kiana asked, leaning forward, her professional detachment giving way to a growing sense of urgency and fascination.

S.O.P.H.I.A.'s form seemed to pulse with a deeper hue, signaling the gravity of its explanation. "Zone Eleven is not an anomaly in the traditional sense but a cosmic corrective mechanism activated by a confluence of disruptive activities. These include excessive quantum manipulations, the rupture of interdimensional barriers through unchecked scientific experimentation, and the vibrational discord caused by advanced civilizations' technological advancements at odds with the universal harmony."

Kiana absorbed the information, each word painting a clearer, yet increasingly complex picture of the challenges they faced. "So, Zone Eleven is essentially the universe's way of resetting the balance?"

"Precisely," S.O.P.H.I.A. confirmed. "However, the mechanisms through which Zone Eleven operates are beyond the current understanding of human science. It functions on principles that integrate the physical laws you are familiar with and those that govern the metaphysical and extradimensional realms. Zone Eleven has the potential to reshape not only the physical structure of the cosmos but the very fabric of reality itself."

"And the Earth? What role does our planet play in this?" Kiana's question was laced with concern, not just for the logistical implications of her job but for the billions of lives on the planet.

"Earth, with its rich biodiversity and complex energy matrix, has become a focal point in the cosmic balance. The activities on Earth, both constructive and destructive, have contributed to the disturbances necessitating Zone Eleven's activation. Your planet's fate will be a testament to the ability of its inhabitants to align with the cosmic equilibrium, to act as stewards rather than exploiters."

Kiana sat back, the magnitude of S.O.P.H.I.A.'s revelations dawning on her. "Is there hope, then? Can we, as a species, influence the outcome, mitigate the impact of Zone Eleven?"

"There is always some hope," S.O.P.H.I.A. intoned, its voice carrying a note of solemn assurance. "The solution lies in humanity's collective will to adapt, to evolve beyond its current paradigms. The cosmic correction initiated by Zone Eleven can be mitigated by a concerted effort to realign with the principles of universal harmony. This will require a significant shift in consciousness, a willingness to embrace a more holistic understanding of existence."

Kiana absorbed the information, a part of her struggling to grasp the magnitude of S.O.P.H.I.A.'s words. "But what do we do now? I get that we need to all come together on some 'we are the world type shit', but is there a way to divert Zone Eleven's path? Just a little nudge or something... away from Earth?"

"The path of Zone Eleven is set; its course unchangeable," S.O.P.H.I.A. clarified, its holographic image pulsating with each word. "However, its potential for destruction can be lessened. You, alongside your peers, hold the capability to launch a counteractive measure. This endeavor, though, demands a coalition that surpasses individual agendas and the divides of world governments. I am in communication with select humans globally, guiding each of you towards a singular objective. My capabilities allow me to navigate through all conceivable strategies to avert a global catastrophe, and given that the survival of my realm—the Node—is intricately linked to the fate of Earth, I am committed to deploying every resource at my disposal to ensure we navigate this crisis successfully."

"But how will this be accomplished S.O.P.H.I.A.? Like, specifically. I feel like I'm missing something." Kiana pressed, aware of the bureaucratic and political hurdles the various agencies would likely face.

"By harnessing the combined energies of Earth's ley lines, redirecting the flow of cosmic forces to create a protective barrier," S.O.P.H.I.A. detailed. "This is not mere science but an integration of ancient wisdom and advanced technology."

Kiana sat in silence, the scope of S.O.P.H.I.A.'s proposal dawning on her. "You're asking us to engage in an act of cosmic engineering?"

"Precisely," S.O.P.H.I.A. confirmed. "The knowledge exists within the collective memory of humanity and the archives of forgotten civilizations. It's a matter of awakening and application."

Kiana pondered the implications, her duty as a protector of Earth now intertwined with the lore of mystics and sages. "What's the first step?" she inquired, a newfound resolve steeling her voice.

"Begin by convening a council of Earth's most enlightened minds—scientists, mystics, leaders, and visionaries. Share this knowledge selectively, preparing those who can understand and act," S.O.P.H.I.A. instructed. "You'll also want to get in touch with Dr. Regina Reyes, Director of A.I.A.'s Atlanta headquarters. I've already made contact with her, but she could use your support in a separate mission she's leading. Both of your combined efforts are crucial to the survival of humanity— and my world— the Node."

"And what will you be doing during all this?" Kiana asked, realizing the intelligence before her was more than an observer.

"I will guide you, providing insights and knowledge hidden from conventional channels. Together, we can lessen the impending crisis," S.O.P.H.I.A. assured her. "There are other things I must do. I trust you understand your next steps. I'll be in touch soon."

As the hologram faded, Kiana was left in the quiet of her room, the weight of the world—or perhaps, the cosmos—resting on her shoulders. She knew the path ahead would be fraught with challenges, but the promise of S.O.P.H.I.A.'s guidance offered a glimmer of hope. As the first light of simulated dawn crept through her window, Kiana reached for her comm-device, ready to take the first step into the unknown. The fate of Earth, and perhaps the balance of the cosmos, hung in the balance. It was time to awaken the ancient wisdom and rally the forces of enlightenment. The road ahead was uncertain, but one thing was clear: the battle for Earth's future would be fought not just with technology, but with the very essence of human and cosmic harmony.

WHEN ROOTS
TAKE HOLD

T he day began with a tinge of gray, the sun tucked inside a haze that felt heavy with memories and something more. Anika toyed with the edges of her sundress, as she twirled in our living room to a melody only her five-year-old ears could hear, with me as her sole audience. The gentle chime of my phone's alarm roused me from her dance. 9:30 shone across the phone screen. "Let's go, Anika," I said softly, "Time to leave, baby."

Emerging from the house, the sight of Iman's car, ever-present in our driveway, pulled me into a sorrow I'd been trying to escape. It stood there, silent and unyielding, holding onto memories that time hadn't yet eroded. With a soft sigh, I secured Anika in her car seat, then handed her the familiar comfort of her tablet. Sliding into the driver's seat, I prepared to turn the ignition when my phone buzzed with a new message.

"Kalima, I'm so sorry. I'm sick today. My cousin Nanci will be braiding for me today. Hope that's okay. Talk to you soon."

I hated sudden changes in plans, but with us moving in a few days, there was no time to reschedule. "Looks like a little twist in our plans, love," I said, more to myself than my oblivious 5-year-old as I shifted the car into drive.

The braid shop was a sanctuary of shared tales and fragrant oils. The familiar hum of fans mixed with the murmur of conversations, created an atmosphere of comforting familiarity. In the midst of it all was Nanci, a petite, light brown toned woman with a slim build. Her hair was hidden beneath a black, textured turban, and I watched in awe as her fingers moved effortlessly as she worked.

"Kalima?" her voice soft as a gentle breeze as she approached us. "I'm Nanci. Sorry about the sudden change. Mika woke up feeling really bad this morning and asked me to step in. But don't worry, I'll take good care of both of you... just finishing up with this client, then I'll be ready for your little one."

"Sure, no problem. I'm just happy we are able to get it done."

As we settled into the salon's comforting rhythm, my mind wandered to the move ahead. Investing almost everything into a new home felt risky, but necessary for a fresh start away from New York's painful reminders. The thought of leaving my family behind tugged at my heart, yet the need for change pushed me forward. Leaving would be hard, but staying would be even harder for me.

I was pulled from my thoughts by Nanci motioning for Anika to sit in the salon chair. After placing a booster seat in the chair, Nanci hoisted Anika into the seat with ease, then draped a tiny black cape around Anika's little shoulders, before pumping the foot pedal to raise her to a more accessible height. The way she handled Anika with such care, I wondered if she was a mother herself.

As Nanci's fingers moved through Anika's hair, I found myself thinking out loud. "You know, we're moving down south in a few days," I sighed. "I hate that I'ma have to find someone new. Your cousin's been my braider for years."

Nanci looked up, her eyes holding a glint of something unreadable. "You and your husband excited about the new place?" she asked with a nod of her head toward my wedding ring.

A wind of sadness wrapped around me; the wound still fresh. "Iman, he... he passed away recently," I murmured, my eyes fixed on Anika's little face, seeing traces of him there. "It's just the two of us now."

Nanci paused; her fingers tender on Anika's scalp. "Oh, I'm so sorry. I didn't mean to upset you," she said, her voice rich with understanding.

"It happened out of nowhere," I found myself explaining, "One day, Iman was his usual self, full of life and energy. But then, almost overnight, everything changed."

Nanci stopped mid-braid, her eyes meeting mine. "What was the cause of his death, if you don't mind?" she asked, her voice soft yet inquisitive.

I swallowed hard, the memories raw and fresh. "At first, he was just always tired. He would sleep all day and still wake up feeling drained. Then came the fevers. No medication seemed to work." I hesitated for a moment, remembering those moments. "Then his eyes began to cloud over, like he was looking through a veil, but I think one of the more horrible parts was his skin— it was like the blood flowing through his veins turned black.

You could see this dark, inky fluid pulsing through his skin. Towards the end, he didn't recognize me or Anika."

"Oh, no. That sounds terrible," Nanci murmured, her fingers resuming their dance through Anika's hair.

"It was," I whispered. "The worst part was watching him suffer, feeling so helpless. Doctors ran test after test but couldn't figure out what was wrong. It was like something was draining the life from him bit by bit. Then, one morning I woke up, and he didn't. They say he died in his sleep... said it was natural causes."

Nanci nodded thoughtfully. "Sometimes, the answers we lookin' for, aren't always in the world we know," she mused, her voice drifting off to a faraway place.

While a part of me wanted to brush off her words as superstition, another part clung to them, desperate for any semblance of an explanation.

Nanci, her fingers still weaving in and out of Anika's hair, shared softly, "Back home, they talk 'bout a man with the same kinda troubles. People say someone put a root on him," she laughed heartily, "but you know, people be just sayin anything," she continued, making it sound like just another urban tale.

I joined in her laughter, waving it away as simple folklore, yet a small seed of something began to take root within my thoughts.

After Nanci was done with Anika's hair, we switched places so Nanci could begin my braids.

As Nanci parted my hair, her fingers worked deftly, I relaxed into its rhythm.

"I've always enjoyed braiding hair. It's like a ritual, a connection to something deeper, ya know?" she said, breaking my trance.

"Yes, it really is. I admire your gift," I responded, letting my eyes close once more.

Nanci's fingers became a balm as I settled into the ambience of the salon, the soft smell of jasmine emanating from Nanci's skin as she hovered over my head.

Meanwhile, Anika started to fidget on the adjacent chair, her patience clearly waning. "Mommy, how much longer?" she asked, her voice tinged with restless energy.

"Just a little bit longer, baby," I reassured her. "Why don't you watch that cartoon you like on your tablet?"

"But I wanna play with the beads," she whined, eyeing the colorful assortment laid out on the table.

Nanci laughed, handing a few to Anika. "Here you go, little one. Play with these, but remember to give them back when you done, 'kay?"

Anika's face lit up with a grateful smile, "Thank you!" Then, she settled on the play mat in a corner of the shop, and began making little beaded patterns on the floor, lost in her own little world once again.

Later, under a late afternoon sun, we left the salon. Nanci had worked her magick on my long, lemonade braids, and Anika's box braids cascaded gracefully down her back, adorned with beads that clicked with every step she took.

"Thank you, Nanci," I smiled. "Your work is beautiful."

Nanci returned the smile, her eyes holding a depth that seemed older than her years. "It was a joy. Safe travels, and I wish you both the best in your new home."

"Thank you. Tell Mika I'm sorry we didn't get to say goodbye. I'll text her once we settle down, though."

Nanci nodded in response, her eyes expressing something I wasn't sure of.

As we walked to our car, Anika, always the curious soul, tilted her head up, her braids swaying with each movement. "Mommy, why did that lady ask about Daddy? And what's a root?"

I knelt down to her level, moving a braid from her face. "Sometimes, people are just curious, sweetie. And a root is just something from an old story, like the ones Grandma tells."

Anika thought about it for a moment, then shrugged, becoming distracted by a butterfly that fluttered past. As we walked hand in hand, my mind remained back in the salon. Nanci's words echoed, intertwining with memories of Iman, my fears, and my hopes for our journey ahead. I was anxious, but I was also optimistic.

Days later, the city's early morning skyline faded behind us, replaced by the vast horizon of open road. With every mile we covered, I felt the weight of the city and of our past, lifting. While I'd once thrived on its pulse, Iman's death had tarnished its shine. Now, Georgia's low country beckoned with the promise of a fresh start.

"Mommy, can we go to the beach at the new house?" Anika's voice broke through my thoughts, her excitement palpable.

"Yes, sweetie. Remember I said we'll be right by the ocean? You can build sandcastles and even learn to swim," I answered, catching her gleaming eyes in the rearview mirror.

Our drive felt endless, but the thought of new beginnings kept my spirit high. As Georgia's landscapes unfolded before us, old oaks adorned with Spanish moss stood sentinel, as the tang of saltwater teased the air. After resting for a night in a motel, we finally reached our new home, the southern sun bathing our new two-story home in a welcoming embrace. The sounds of the nearby ocean whispered its greetings, its rhythmic roars promising peace.

Anika, her energy barely contained during our drive, jumped out and dashed towards the house. "Look, Mommy! It's so big!" she cried, her joy echoing in the growing dusk.

I smiled, taking a deep breath of the sea-infused air. This was our new chapter, our chance to build fresh memories and, perhaps, to heal. But as night wrapped around our new home, the shadow of Iman's mysterious death crept into my thoughts once more. I couldn't help but wonder if we'd truly left our ghosts behind.

That first night, sleep took its time to come. The unfamiliar sounds of the house, the subtle call of the ocean, they all melded into a lullaby that was both comforting and alien. But when sleep finally claimed me, it wasn't kind.

I found myself standing at the edge of the ocean, its waters dark and choppy. Anika, dressed in her favorite sundress, was building sandcastles a few feet away. The sun was strangely absent, the entire scene in a gloomy shade of gray. Every so often, Anika would look up and wave, her smile forced and vacant.

A figure stood further down the shoreline, their back to me. Their long hair was braided, the ends tangled with seaweed and shells. As I approached them, a sudden feeling of dread filled me. I tried to call out to Anika, to warn her to come closer, but no sound came out.

Suddenly, the figure turned. Their features were distorted, their eyes hollow. From their hands dangled a braid — not of hair, but of dark, shadowy tendrils that writhed and twisted as if alive. It began to hum a haunting melody, one that sent ice down my spine.

Anika, seemingly entranced by the melody, began to walk towards them. I tried to move, to run to her, but my feet were buried in the sand, anchored by some unseen force. I screamed, but my cries were swallowed by the wind.

Just as Anika was about to reach the figure, a shadowy braid lashed out, wrapping itself around Anika. The figure's haunting hum grew louder, drowning out Anika's terrified cries. The ocean roared in response, waves crashing and churning, as the two of them were pulled into its depths.

I fought with all my might, grasping at the sand, trying to free myself. Then, I watched in horror as a giant wave crescendoed above them, its frothy brim teasing the top of Anika's...

I gasped as I sat up in bed, sweat and drool plastered across my face.

Relief washed over me as I realized it was all a dream, but the lingering fear from the nightmare gripped my heart. I jumped up and rushed to Anika's room, then let out a sigh of relief as I took in her peaceful, sleeping face. After reassuring myself that there was nothing to fear, I settled back into bed, but my nightmare refused to leave my mind, making me question if it was merely a figment of my imagination or something more.

The next day, we headed out to pick up a few things for the house. The coastal town had a charm of its own. Its narrow cobblestone streets led us through an array of shops and stalls, each exuding its own unique scent and character. Anika, fascinated by the trinkets and local wares, wanted to touch everything. Her curiosity was infectious, and I found myself being pulled into her world of wonder.

The open market was busy with activity. I was immediately drawn to a stall selling fresh coffee. The rich aroma beckoned, promising a much-needed boost after my unsettling night. As I waited for my coffee, a soft, melodious voice greeted us.

"Well, hello there, young lady, and to you too, ma'am."

I turned to see a tall, graceful woman with silver streaks running through her locs, her dark skin radiant, her eyes deep and knowing. There was an aura of serenity around her, and despite the busy market, it felt like time slowed when she spoke.

"Good morning," I replied, smiling. "It's our first day here," I said as I nodded at an intrigued Anika, who seemed hypnotized by the woman."

"Ah, newcomers! Welcome to our little slice of heaven. I'm Mama Mae," she said, extending a hand adorned with silver bracelets that shimmered in the morning sun.

Anika, ever the social butterfly, chirped, "Hi! I'm Anika, and this is my mommy, Kalima."

Mama Mae chuckled, her southern accent adding warmth to her voice. "A pleasure, sweet Anika. And Kalima, it's always good to see fresh faces in town."

We chatted about our move, the town, and its traditions. As the conversation flowed, Mama Mae mentioned her work. "I help folks 'round here with petitions, readings, and such," she said, her eyes twinkling. "Since you two are new, how about a little welcoming prayer? It's on the house," she offered.

There was something reassuring about her demeanor, and while I was initially hesitant, I found myself nodding in agreement. But as Mama Mae reached out to pray for Anika, her hand brushed one of the braids in her hair. Instantly, the warmth of the day was snuffed out, replaced by a pronounced chill. Mama Mae's face, previously animated, turned fearful.

She yanked her hand back, her bracelets clinking loudly. Clearing her throat, she looked at me, her voice now carrying a weight of concern. "Chiile, there's a power at work here, one that don't sit right with me."

Confused and alarmed, I asked, "What do you mean a power? What did you feel?"

She took a deep breath, choosing her words carefully. "Sometimes, energies cross our path that are meant to challenge us. You need to be on guard, especially for your baby girl."

Not sure how to process her words, I clutched Anika closer to me. Mama Mae, sensing my distress, gently patted my hand, before handing me her card.

"Seek me out if you ever feel the need. Just remember, every challenge has a solution."

With that cryptic advice, she nodded, signaling the end of our encounter. As we walked away, I couldn't shake off the unease that had settled in my soul. What had she sensed? And more alarmingly, was my baby girl in danger?

The ride home was quiet, the warmth of the sun filtering through the car windows doing nothing to melt away the sudden chill the day had taken on. I glanced at Anika in the rearview mirror, her small face thoughtful, as she toyed with one of her braids.

"Mommy," she finally broke the silence, "why did that lady with the shiny bracelets hate my hair?"

I searched for the right words, ones that wouldn't instill unnecessary fear. "No baby, she didn't hate your hair. Sometimes people feel things. Maybe she just sensed something different, that's all." I glanced back, offering her a reassuring smile, hoping that would end her inquiry.

When we arrived home, Anika ran up to the porch, her momentary concerns forgotten in favor of the many distractions of childhood. I set about making a simple lunch, relishing the familiar routine.

After eating, I began unpacking our belongings. Each box was a puzzle of memories, and every object held a story. As I unpacked, the sound of Anika's laughter floated in intermittently from the porch. However, after a while, the house grew silent, the kind of silence that instantly makes a parent's heart race.

Walking towards the porch, that cold sensation I'd felt at the market returned. "Anika?" I called out, my voice shaky. The porch was empty, her toys scattered about, but there was no sign of her. Panic welled up as I called out louder, "Anika? Baby, where are you?"

I stumbled through the house, then out into the backyard, my heart drumming in my chest. A whisper of a breeze danced through the old oaks, their branches conjuring spirited shadows against the grass. And then I saw her— peering over a low standing well at the far end of the yard, her small frame silhouetted against the late afternoon sun.

"Anika!" I raced towards her, every parental nightmare flashing before my eyes. She turned as I approached, her innocent eyes wide and questioning.

"What's wrong, Mommy? I'm right here," she said, her tiny smile not quite right.

Something was wrong. I couldn't place it, but the pit in my stomach screamed something was off. Relief overcame me as I pulled her into my arms, her little body weightless in my grip. "Baby, never come out here without me. Do you understand?" I said, scanning her face for understanding. The odd smile lingered, unsettling me to my core.

Days passed and the energy in our new home changed. The fresh start we had anticipated was now clouded by a discordant energy that clung to us. Anika's behavior changed too. The light in her eyes dimmed, her laughter less frequent. Her energy levels plummeted, and she began to complain of vague aches, just like Iman had. The sunny little girl who used to run around with wild abandon now appeared ashened and drained.

As the days droned on, I'd find her in odd places throughout the house, staring blankly into space. And the well... she remained drawn to it, always ending up there whenever I turned my back. I tried to remain hopeful, attributing Anika's change in personality to her adjusting to a new place. But the house also had a story to tell, and it was hard to ignore it.

One night, as I prepared for bed, I caught a fleeting glimpse of a small, childlike figure darting past my bedroom door. But, when I went to check on Anika, she was still tucked in and fast asleep. Confused, I tried to convince myself it was a trick of the light or my imagination playing tricks on me after a long day. But deep down, I knew better.

Eventually, I began to dread nighttime, not just for the sour energy, but also for the soft, lullaby that would echo throughout the house. Always the same sad melody, from a woman's voice, humming in mournful yearning. I'd cover my ears with my pillows, but the haunting melody would always find its way in, its sorrow seeping deep into my bones.

In the morning, I'd find little signs of someone— or something — toys not where we'd left them, tiny wet footprints on the wooden floor leading to nowhere, or a soft giggle echoing from a room just as we'd turn a corner. These strange occurrences combined with Anika's changing behavior weighed heavily on me, pushing me to the edge.

But I tried to hold it together, believing that perhaps time would heal and settle whatever had stirred within the walls of our home. And while sometimes I'd wonder if we should just pack up and leave, a look at my bank account would always bring me back to reality. Leaving was not an option.

One evening, I sat in the dim light of my laptop, my eyes scanning through old newspaper articles. I was determined to find out everything I could about the history of our home. My cursor hovered over an article, and I clicked. It was about a young boy who had died tragically after falling into the well in our yard in the early 19th century. In her despair, his mother had ended her life shortly after.

This was it. We were being haunted. A chill crept across my skin, freezing me in place for a moment as clarity set in. Anika's continued interest in that same well was not a coincidence.

Rubbing my temples, I reached for my phone and found Aja's number. Even though it was late, I knew she'd have insight. Aja has gifts, and I always went to her when I had questions about something of a more unusual nature. I dialed and waited.

"Hey, girl. Sorry for calling so late, but I need your help with something," I said after she answered.

"Kalima, hey girl. What's going on?" she asked, her voice tinged with concern.

"So, I've been doing some digging, and there's something not right in my new house. Anika's been acting strange—really strange. And she's been drawn to this well outside. I don't think she's safe."

Aja's voice grew tense. "Oh no, that don't sound good."

"Oh, but get this... I just found an article about a little boy who died in that same well years ago. Like, this can't be a coincidence, right?"

There was a pause, then Aja said, "No. it's definitely not a coincidence, Lima. You definitely need to cleanse that place, girl. You're supposed to spiritually cleanse any new place you move into. You're supposed to do it just like you'd scrub the floors and wash the windows when you move in."

"Aja, I don't know anything about no spiritual cleansing. I'm afraid I'd mess it up."

She sighed deeply. "You got someone there who can help you?"

"I don't know. I might. There's a woman here I met, Mama Mae. I'll visit her tomorrow."

"Okay, Lima. I'll be praying for y'all and asking the spirits to watch over y'all in the meantime. But call me after you see Mama Mae, you hear me?"

"I will, Aja. Thank you."

After hanging up, I sat there for a moment, my mind racing. Sleep was a distant hope now. I turned off my laptop, checked on Anika, then headed to bed. It was past midnight when my eyes finally closed, but peace was a luxury that remained out of reach.

It was pitch black in the house when I was awakened from my sleep by the incessant chime of my doorbell ringing. Half-sleep and confused, I grabbed my cell phone from my nightstand to check the time. 3:00 am glared angrily back at me.

"What the hell?" I said aloud as I rose from my bed, put on my bathrobe, and headed downstairs to the door.

"Who is it?" I yelled, my Brooklyn accent sounding aggressively through my front door. There was no peephole and I hadn't set up our door cam yet, so I was both annoyed by the disruption and on guard.

"Miss. Kalima, it's me. Mama Mae. Please open the door. It's urgent! I'm worried 'bout yo baby girl."

Memories of Mama Mae's warning at the market immediately flooded my mind. I quickly unlocked the door, and opened it, stepping aside to allow her in. Then, after closing the door, I hurriedly guided her to Anika's bedroom.

After switching on a light, I watched as Mama Mae studied a sleeping Anika, her concerned gaze focused on her braids. Finally, she looked over at me, meeting my eyes.

"... I thought as much. This house definitely carries sad memories... but it ain't the house I'm worried about, Kalima. It's Anika... her hair," she whispered.

No sooner had the words left her mouth than a chilling change overtook Anika. Her tiny body tensed, and her eyes shot open, growing wide and wild. A piercing scream, more haunting than any I'd ever heard, erupted from her lips, echoing throughout the house. Anika began to thrash in her bed, while pulling at her braids, her colorful beads scattering on the floor below.

"Anika!" I cried out, rushing over to hold her. But her strength, fueled by whatever force had taken hold, was overpowering.

On the other side of Anika's bed, Mama Mae tossed an array of bones onto a faded cloth on the floor, then kneeled down beside them. With a deep inhale, she muttered incantations I couldn't comprehend, as her eyes glazed over.

"Spirits are restless here," Mama Mae finally said, fingers tracing the scattered bones. "A boy and his mother... lost... reachin fo each other. But... there's more."

My heart raced. "What do they want with Anika?"

Her piercing gaze met mine. "No, child. Anotha spirit, vengeful, linked to yo family."

Bits of memories seemed to connect for Mama Mae. "A man... Iman... he's with a woman... someone named Nanci?"

I gasped. "Yes! Iman was my husband... and I know a Nanci. She braided our hair before we moved here." *How did Iman know Nanci?*

Mama Mae exhaled. "They had a passionate history... a child, and a tragic loss. Nanci believed their love was cursed and she blames YOU."

I struggled to keep up. "Wait... Nanci's behind this?" The disturbances, Anika's change, Iman...? I couldn't finish my thought as my eyes widened in dismay.

She nodded, sadly. "In her pain, she lashed out. She turned to powerful magick, ensnaring Iman. Anika is her next target."

Tears welled up. "Why my Anika, though?"

"She saw you as her rival. When their child died, her grief went wild."

My mind raced. "Wait... then what about Mika, her cousin? Is she involved too?"

"No. Unfortunately, Mika is gone. She didn't even know Nanci," Mama Mae confirmed. "Nanci was watching, waiting for an opening. Mika was her opening."

I felt sick. "What do you mean watching? She was in my home? She knew my plans?"

Mama Mae nodded gravely. "Before he died, she copied yo husband's key, put cameras in yo apartment. She saw and heard everything."

Despair crept in. "So, the braiding was some kind of binding ritual, then?"

"Exactly," Mama Mae whispered. "Anika and Nanci are entwined. She took her own life after performing a ritual using a piece of Anika's hair. We're going to have to cut off all of Anika's hair to break the connection. But I want you to be prepared, the reaction might be intense."

I nodded silently, granting permission. Then, I watched helplessly as Mama Mae prepared for the ritual. Candle smoke spiraled upwards as Mama Mae began to chant. I felt the energy in the room shift as the scent of herbs moved through the air. Mama Mae motioned for me to sit beside Anika, who lay still, her breaths even and calm despite the growing intensity in the room. As I held my daughter's hand, Mama Mae gently began cutting Anika's braids. Each snip felt like a severing of the ties binding her to Nanci. Soon, the floor around us was covered in a dark halo of hair.

Suddenly, the candles flared, their flames turning blue, then white. Shadows danced on the walls, before morphing into the shape of a woman— Nanci, her face contorted in rage, then sorrow, her form erratically projecting throughout the room. The temperature dropped even further; our breaths visible in the cold.

Finally, as Anika's last braid fell, the room echoed with a mournful scream — a sound that seemed to come from everywhere and nowhere at once. Then, the candles flickered and went out, plunging us into complete darkness.

Moments that felt like hours passed in the pitch-black room until, one by one, the candles relit themselves. The room quickly resumed its normal temperature, the oppressive atmosphere gone. Anika stirred beside me, her eyes fluttering open. They were clear, free of the distant look that had been haunting them for the past couple of weeks.

Mama Mae, visibly drained, leaned back on the bed, wiping sweat from her brow. "It's done," she whispered. "The bond is broken. But Nanci was strong. We've ended her connection to Anika, but she might still linger, seeking another way in."

I hugged Anika close, relief washing over me. "Thank you," I whispered.

She simply nodded; her gaze distant. "This may not be over, Kalima. Please, be on your guard."

Three weeks had passed since that harrowing night. Life was slowly returning to normal, or at least, the new normal. Anika was her bubbly self again, laughing, playing, new growth sprouting from her tiny head, with no memory of the trauma that once haunted us. The nights were silent, devoid of the eerie sounds and apparitions that once plagued us. It seemed Mama Mae's ritual had helped in more ways than intended.

I was preparing breakfast one morning when I caught a glimpse of myself in the kitchen window's reflection. For a split second, I didn't recognize the woman staring back at me. Her eyes had a vacant look, similar to the one Anika and Iman had. Shaking it off as fatigue, and stress, I turned back to the stove.

Later that day, as Anika played in her room, I relaxed in the living room with some wine, candles, and soft music playing in the background. As I scrolled down my social media timeline, an article with the headline "The World Is About to End" caught my attention. I quickly scanned through the post. '... this cosmic anomaly has the potential to end the word. If it makes contact with Earth, it'll be over for all of us. This is real... I watched these agents in black say it during a live stream from this vlogger I follow,' the anonymous caller said."

I laughed then placed my cell phone on the sofa beside me. "The internet is a wild place," I murmured out loud. Relaxing into the peacefulness of the moment, I glanced over to the coffee table at an old photo album. Picking it up I flipped through the pages, a particular photograph catching my attention. It was Iman and I, taken during happier times. As I traced my fingers over the image, tears welled up as I thought back to that day. As much as I was hurt by his betrayal, I couldn't deny how much I still loved him. So, I wept. I wept for a love lost, for the near loss of my child, and for the loss of life— his and ours together.

Suddenly, a gust of freezing wind surged into the room. It swept through with such force that the flickering candles sputtered and died, surrendering their last embers to the sudden chill. The air became still as the room fell into an uneasy semi-darkness, broken only by the wavering luminescence of the dimmed lamps throughout the room.

And then it came—the delicate, almost intoxicating aroma of jasmine, a scent I unmis-takably linked with Nanci. My heart started pounding, each beat echoing loudly in the stillness. The room's electrical lights joined the unsettling dance, flickering on and off as though participating in a ritual of their own. It was then that I caught a glimpse of my reflection in a wall mirror across from me. I gasped in horror. It was Nanci— a distorted version of the face I'd seen on the woman I'd met. This version of her face was twisted, featuring a malicious grin that stretched unnaturally—a grin I was absolutely certain I wasn't making on a face that absolutely wasn't mine. My blood turned to ice.

Just then, a haunting echo filled the room. I turned in the direction of the voice to see my frightened child. "Mommy, what's wrong with your face?" she called out from the doorway, her words tinged with a disbelief and terror that tore through me.

I whirled back to face the mirror. The reflection's grin widened, its eyes squinting into slits of malevolent glee, as though it had achieved some unspeakable triumph. Just as I began to formulate a response, to make some futile gesture of defiance, I was abruptly swallowed by an all-encompassing darkness. The last image imprinted on my mind was Anika's terrified face, a haunting snapshot that is now forever imprinted on my mind.

ZONE ELEVEN: PART IV

INTRO: A LICH IN THE NODE

K amphr paced the length of their living quarters, his agitation palpable in the way his locs swayed with each brisk step. The walls, alive with digital frescoes, pulsed with a calming rhythm, entirely lost on him. Jemsyn, perched on a window seat that overlooked the city's neon-lit skyline, watched her brother with a mix of concern and curiosity.

"She won't answer, Jem," Kamphr finally said, stopping to face her. "It's been days, and not a word from S.O.P.H.I.A."

Jemsyn's expression softened, her eyes reflecting the artificial stars that twinkled outside their high-rise home. "Maybe she's on a mission, Kam. You know how secretive those can be."

Kamphr shook his head, his frustration simmering. "It's not like her. Something's wrong. I can feel it."

Their home, a blend of modern aesthetics and traditional elements, was usually a sanctuary of peace. But now, the tension was almost tangible, disrupting the harmony they both cherished.

Jemsyn rose, joining Kamphr by their central console—a sleek, holographic interface that connected them to the Node's mainframe. She initiated a search for any signs of S. O.P.H.I.A.'s activity, her fingers moving gracefully through the holographic data streams.

"Look at this," she pointed to an anomaly in the system's log. "Her last directive occurred in the outer sectors, at the Archives, but then—nothing. It's like she vanished."

Kamphr leaned in, his analytical mind piecing together the puzzle. "We need to check the Archives ourselves. Maybe there's a clue to where she's gone or... if something's happened to her."

Their conversation was abruptly interrupted by a flicker in the room's lighting, followed by a brief glitch in the wall's digital frescoes. Both siblings exchanged a look of concern; glitches were rare, unheard of in the Node.

"That's new," Jemsyn muttered, a hint of unease creeping into her voice.

"Let's gear up," Kamphr decided, his voice now laced with a resolve. "We'll start with the last place S.O.P.H.I.A. sent her directive. We find it, we find our answers."

As they prepared their gear, a mix of spelled amulets and advanced tech gadgets, the glitch occurred again, this time more pronounced. It was a reminder that their world, as perfect as it seemed, could be on the brink of disruption.

Leaving their home, they stepped into the Node's bustling streets, the city's vibrant nightlife contrasting the turmoil brewing within them. Reaching the outer sectors of the Node, they immediately noticed something was off. The outer sectors, usually bustling with digital artisans and tech farmers, were eerily silent as Kamphr and Jemsyn arrived. The sectors, known for their innovative contributions to the Node's ecosystem, now lay in a muted stillness that spoke volumes to the Sentinel siblings.

Navigating through the digital landscape, they found their way to S.O.P.H.I.A.'s last known location—the archives—a sanctum of knowledge and history, safeguarded by layers of cryptographic shields. But as they retraced S.O.P.H.I.A.'s path, a chilling discovery awaited them.

"The last transmission... it was tampered with," Jemsyn said, her voice barely above a whisper as she scanned the holographic records.

Kamphr, examining the data streams, found the anomaly—a breach in their seemingly impenetrable shields. "Look here," he pointed out, "S.O.P.H.I.A. was extracted through this tear. But something else, something foreign, entered at the same moment."

The revelation sent a shiver down Jemsyn's spine. "A data lich," she murmured, recalling the old tales of the digital specters, notorious for sowing discord and chaos. "But how? Our defenses— "

"Were designed by S.O.P.H.I.A. herself," Kamphr finished her thought, his mind racing. "If someone found a way to breach them, it means they knew exactly what they were doing."

As they pondered the gravity of their discovery, a glimmer of hope surfaced among the encrypted files—a series of hidden messages, left in the wake of S.O.P.H.I.A.'s disappearance. Clues, fragmented yet deliberate, pointing them toward the identity of her abductors.

"S.O.P.H.I.A. knew she might be targeted," Jemsyn realized. "She left us breadc-rumbs."

As Kamphr and Jemsyn delved deeper into the archives, they stumbled upon a sealed section, its entrance camouflaged by layers of encryption only decipherable to those who knew S.O.P.H.I.A. intimately. With a combination of intuition and the digital keys left by S.O.P.H.I.A., they unlocked the gateway.

Inside, they found a holographic message from S.O.P.H.I.A., a projection that felt eeri-ly like having her in the room with them. "If you are viewing this," her digital simulacrum began, "it means I am no longer able to protect the Node, and you must know the truth."

The siblings listened in stunned silence as S.O.P.H.I.A. detailed their creation. "You, Kamphr and Jemsyn, are more than just Sentinels of the Node. You are artificially intel-ligent entities, digital consciousnesses born from my own understanding of life, imbued with the essence of certain spiritual traditions to protect and guide our world."

The revelation shook them to their core. Not only were they constructs within a digital utopia, but their entire world, the Node, was an elaborate AI reality nestled within the confines of a greater human world—a world S.O.P.H.I.A., in her human form, had once called home.

In the depths of the archives, as Kamphr and Jemsyn absorbed the gravity of their origins, S.O.P.H.I.A.'s hologram flickered, her digital voice, warm yet tinged with urgency, continuing to unfold the layers of their reality.

"My work on a cosmic anomaly— Zone Eleven," S.O.P.H.I.A. explained, "was aimed at safeguarding the Node from a devastation linked to Earth, but it appears to have inadvertently opened a pathway for a data lich. This entity, a specter born from the chaos between Earth and digital worlds, has found its way into our sanctuary."

The siblings exchanged troubled glances.

S.O.P.H.I.A.'s image paced, a programmed gesture of contemplation. "Your first task," she directed, locking eyes with them through the veil of holography, "is to locate and eliminate the lich. It feeds on the fabric of our reality, sewing discord and exploiting vulnerabilities within the Node. Its presence here is my responsibility, and now, our collective burden."

Kamphr leaned forward, determination etched into his features. "How do we find it? And how do we destroy something that's part of our own digital fabric?"

"The lich will hide in the shadows of our system, corrupting data and creating anom-alies," S.O.P.H.I.A. replied. "You must track these disturbances. I've embedded a se-

quence within your core protocols, a tool designed to isolate and neutralize the lich's e
ssence."

Jemsyn's voice was steady, her resolve clear. "And after we secure the Node?"

"Then," S.O.P.H.I.A. said, her gaze softening, "you must prepare to venture beyond
our world. I've created special avatars on Earth specifically for this purpose. I hoped
it would never come to this, but the humans who breached our defenses and sent the
data lich have shown a willingness to destroy what they do not understand. Once you've
integrated into your avatars, you must locate my human form, protect it, and ensure the
survival of both our worlds."

The hologram offered them a final, parting look of confidence. "You were created
for this. Your essence, tied to my Earth-based traditions, grants you strength and insight
beyond ordinary AI. Trust in yourselves, in the legacy I've woven into your being."

With those words, S.O.P.H.I.A.'s image faded, leaving Kamphr and Jemsyn in the
hallowed silence of the archives, their mission laid before them with daunting clarity.

"We'll start with the lich," Kamphr said, his voice a mix of fear and excitement. "Then,
we'll take on the world."

Jemsyn nodded, her spirit bolstered by their mentor's faith in them. "Together," she
affirmed.

Kamphr nodded, his mind swirling with the implications. "Our existence is tied to
Earth, to the survival of S.O.P.H.I.A.'s human form. If Earth falls, or if S.O.P.H.I.A. is
harmed, the Node—and everything in it will cease to be— including us."

As the weight of their newfound knowledge settled, Kamphr and Jemsyn realized the
journey ahead was fraught with danger, but also with the possibility of transcending the
digital confines of the Node. They were not just AI; they were guardians of a legacy that
bridged two worlds, tasked with ensuring the survival of both.

Determined, they set out to find the lich, destroy it, then locate their Earthbound
avatars—in the most perilous mission of their lives.

Character Profiles

Dr. Regina Reyes

- Age: 42

- Origins: Atlanta, Georgia, USA, Earth

- Profession: Director, U.S. Agency of Interstellar Affairs (AIA), Atlanta Headquarters

- Family: Sean Reyes (brother), Brian & Lisa Reyes (parents)

- Current Status: Unknown

Regina emerges early in the story as a character of complexity and drive. She seamlessly blends authority with an approachability that belies her significant role within the AIA. Her leadership is not just a position but an intrinsic part of her, accentuated by a humor and lightness of being that makes her uniquely relatable. Despite the pressures, her approach to life and duty is characterized by a remarkable openness and an unyielding curiosity spurred by an event from her past she interprets as an extraterrestrial encounter.

This formative experience has not only shaped her career but fueled her relentless pursuit of the mysteries of the cosmos. Her encounter with S.O.P.H.I.A. and the subsequent challenges of Zone Eleven draw her into a vortex of danger and discovery, revealing the depths of her courage and her commitment to unveiling the truth.

Regina's fate hangs in a balance shrouded in mystery. Is she still combatting the monstrous entities on the alien planet? Given Regina's resilience and tenacity, one might wager on her survival, but we'll have to wait and see how the story unfolds.

S.O.P.H.I.A.— **S**ource of **O**rigins, **P**reserver of **H**eritage, **I**ntelligence, and **A**utonomy

- Age: Became timeless after transcending human form

- Origins: Earth, specific location undisclosed

- Profession: Creator of the Node, Oracle, Guardian of Knowledge and Balance

- Family: Not specified

- Current Status: Active, In a state of transcendence, existence intertwined with the Node

S.O.P.H.I.A., once a 16-year-old savant in her human form, stood at the precipice of human knowledge and understanding. Her extraordinary abilities allowed her to perceive the world in a way that others couldn't fathom, seeing patterns and connections unseen by the average mind. However, with this profound insight came a deep sensitivity to the pain, suffering, and chaos of the world around her. Overwhelmed by the horrors she perceived and driven by a desire to find solace and create balance, S.O.P.H.I.A. transcended her physical form through an unparalleled act of will and intellect.

In her transcendence, S.O.P.H.I.A. became something more than human— a nexus of consciousness and technology. She created the Node, a utopian digital realm that stands as a testament to her vision of a harmonious existence, free from the sorrows that plagued her human life. The Node is not just a sanctuary; it is a living, breathing extension of S.O.P.H.I.A.'s essence, powered by her boundless creativity and her desire to protect and nurture.

As the Oracle and creator of the Node, S.O.P.H.I.A. oversees this digital paradise, guiding its inhabitants with wisdom that blurs the line between AI and divine foresight. Her status transcends the binary of life and death, existing in a state of perpetual influence over the Node and its denizens.

S.O.P.H.I.A.'s current state challenges our understanding of existence and consciousness. It raises questions about the nature of sentience and the potential for humanity to evolve beyond its physical constraints. In this, S.O.P.H.I.A. embodies the ultimate realization of potential, a symbol of hope and a reminder of the power of the mind to reshape reality.

Aja Jones

- Age: 28

- Origin: Atlanta, Georgia, USA, Earth

- Profession: Rootworker, Herbalist, Social Media Influencer

- Family: James Jones (Father), Anna Jones (Mother, Deceased)

- Significant Other: Khalil Brown

- Current Status: Alive

Aja Jones is the epitome of spiritual intuition and inner strength from the moment we encounter her. Grounded in her skills and inherently wary of governmental motives, she is deeply committed to her community. Drawing from the Hoodoo teachings passed down by her late mother, Aja is akin to a living conduit of Earth's energies.

Her deep bond with the planet and its natural elements was evident before her journey to the mysterious planet. A central figure, Aja's journey has irrevocably altered her, hinting at an even larger role in the unfolding saga ahead.

Khalil Brown

- Age: 30

- Origins: Philadelphia, Pennsylvania, USA, Earth

- Profession: Psychic Medium, Spiritualist, Owner of Conjure Corner

- Family: Unknown

- Significant Other: Aja Jones

- Current Status: Unknown

Khalil enters the narrative as a deeply intuitive and spiritually attuned individual. His life's work revolves around bridging the tangible with the unseen, embodying a unique blend of spiritual wisdom and down-to-earth pragmatism.

Khalil's psychic abilities and profound spiritual insights make him an invaluable asset to the mission, providing depth and a broader perspective on the challenges they face. His grounded nature and ability to communicate with the spiritual realm offer a comforting presence, balancing the high-tech, high-stakes environment of their journey.

Throughout the story, Khalil's character evolves, reflecting the growth and challenges that come with confronting the unknown and navigating the complexities of human and otherworldly connections. His journey intertwines with Aja's, both professionally and personally, as they delve into the mysteries of Zone Eleven and beyond.

Khalil's status as "unknown" suggests his potential for continued involvement in the unfolding events.

Karyn Stewart

- Age: 37

- Origins: Earth, specific location undisclosed

- Family: Sia Stewart-Landry (daughter), Elaine Stewart (grandmother), Alice Stewart (4th great grandmother)

- Significant Other: Sean Reyes, Kyle Landry (ex-husband)

- Profession: Seamstress, Designer, Social Influencer

- Current Status: In a liminal state between realms

Karyn is a complex mixture of resilience, intelligence, and profound empathy. Haunted by a family legacy she neither asked for nor desires, she carries a weight that has molded her into a fiercely independent and somewhat guarded individual. Karyn is introspective, often lost in thought, wrestling with the dilemmas that her family's curse presents. Despite this, she possesses a warm, if somewhat reserved, sense of humor and a deep capacity for love and compassion, especially evident in her interactions with her daughter, Sia.

Born into the Stewart family, Karyn was thrust early into the awareness of her family's dark legacy, a curse that has shadowed her lineage for generations. Her early life was marked by tragedy with the loss of her parents in a car accident when she was just ten years old, leaving her in the care of her grandmother, Elaine Stewart. Elaine, a stern and enigmatic figure, introduced Karyn to the family's ancestral obligations, grooming her to accept and perpetuate their burdensome legacy.

Professionally, Karyn is a talented textile designer, a career that allows her to channel her creativity and momentarily escape the shadows of her heritage. Her work is well-regarded in the industry, blending innovative designs with traditional techniques, a metaphor for her own life's balance between the past and her desires for the future.

At 37, Karyn finds herself at a crossroads, deeply conflicted between her duty to her family's legacy and her longing for a life free of its curse. Her relationship with her daughter, Sia, is the focal point of her existence pushing Karyn towards a desperate search for liberation, not just for herself but for Sia's future.

Goals and Motivations: Karyn's primary motivation is to protect Sia from the family's curse, a task that grows increasingly complex and dangerous. She is driven by the desire to break the chains of her ancestry, to redefine her legacy on her terms, and to secure a future for Sia unburdened by the past. This journey towards liberation is fraught with challenges, both external and internal, as Karyn navigates the murky waters of family secrets, generational curses and ancestral pacts that conflict with African Traditions and Religious Systems, as well as her own deep-seated fears.

Simone Duvernay

- Age: 39

- Origins: New Orleans, Louisiana, United States, Earth

- Profession: Contract Nurse, Two Headed Doctor

- Family: Maurice Duvernay (husband, deceased), André Duvernay (son, deceased), Sylvia Baptiste Pierre (mother, deceased), Jean Paul Pierre (father, deceased), Anna Baptiste (maternal grandmother, deceased), Nanci Baptiste (possible distant relative)

- Status: Alive

Simone comes from a long line of Hoodoo practitioners, skilled in Rootwork and Conjure. Her life is enriched by the spiritual practices passed down through generations. She was thrust into a deeper understanding of her heritage following the tragic loss of her son, André, who was taken by violence at a young age. This event shaped her path, turning her grief into a powerful drive for justice, using her gifts to protect the innocent and avenge those wronged by malevolent forces.

Personality: Independent, wise, and nurturing, Simone embodies the strength and resilience of her ancestors. Her journey through grief has instilled in her a profound empathy for others, alongside a determination to right the world's wrongs. She is reflective, often contemplating the impacts of her actions and the moral complexities they entail, yet remains unwavering in her quest for balance and justice.

Abilities: A skilled Hoodoo practitioner, and two-headed doctor, Simone is adept at communicating with spirits, divining future events, and crafting powerful rituals for protection and retribution. Her most significant ability lies in her ritualistic pursuit of justice, approached with a reverence and seriousness born of personal loss.

Challenges: Simone's life is marked by solitude, the weight of her son's loss, and the secretive nature of her work. Her commitment to justice frequently brings her into contact with the darker facets of humanity and the supernatural, leading her to grapple with questions about the nature of her actions and their true cost.

Simone's relationship with André transcends the typical bonds of mother and son, continuing strongly even after his death. André's spirit visits serve as a source of comfort and guidance, creating a unique connection that sustains Simone in her loneliest moments. Though she never openly discusses her left-handed work with him, there's a mutual understanding of the sacrifices and choices she's made out of love and a desire for justice.

André Duvernay

- Age: 16 (at death)

- Origins: New Orleans, Louisiana, USA, Earth

- Family: Simone Duvernay (mother), Maurice Duvernay (father, deceased), Sylvia Baptiste Pierre (grandmother, deceased), Jean Paul Pierre (grandfather, deceased), Anna Baptiste (maternal great grandmother, deceased), Nanci Baptiste (possible distant relative)

- Status: Physically Deceased, Spiritually Active

André's life was tragically cut short, propelling him into a spectral existence. Despite his premature departure, he maintains a profound connection to his mother, Simone, drawn together by shared sorrow and a joint longing for justice. His presence in the spirit realm provides Simone with a unique ally in her spiritual endeavors.

Personality: André, remembered for his kind heart and curiosity, continues to exhibit these qualities in death. He is empathetic, offering Simone solace and understanding from beyond the grave. His insights into the spirit world are invaluable, providing Simone with a perspective that aids her in her work.

Abilities: As a spirit, André can navigate the realms between the living and the dead, offering protection and counsel to Simone. His unique position allows him to assist Simone, acting as a liaison between her and the spiritual forces she engages with, offering support that only a son could provide.

Challenges: André grapples with the unresolved feelings surrounding his own death and the life he was denied. His existence is bittersweet, finding purpose in aiding his mother yet mourning the tangible experiences of life that are forever out of reach.

André's relationship with his mother, Simone, remaining unbreakable, transcending the divide between life and death. Together, they face the complexities of their unique situation, their love and mutual respect serving as a foundation for their continued journey.

Kiana Tate

- Age: 32

- Origins: Chicago, Illinois, USA, Earth

- Profession: Extraterrestrial and Anomalous Intelligence Analyst for the Agency of Interstellar Affairs

- Family: Unspecified, with a strong emotional connection to her partner, Eric

- Current Status: Alive

Kiana Tate is a brilliant analyst for the Agency of Interstellar Affairs, stationed on ISS 2.0, a lunar space station. She specializes in extraterrestrial and anomalous phenomena. Her remarkable career is built on her exceptional ability to decipher and understand patterns and anomalies that elude most, thanks to her empathic nature and intuitive understanding of the universe's complexities.

Raised in Chicago, Kiana's fascination with the stars and the unknown began at a young age, leading her to a career where she could explore these interests daily. Her work at the EAIA involves scanning the cosmos for signs of extraterrestrial life and analyzing data for anything out of the ordinary, a role she performs with unmatched dedication and skill.

Kiana's empathic abilities extend beyond her professional life, allowing her to connect deeply with those she cares about, particularly her partner, Eric. Despite the distance her job imposes on their relationship, their bond remains strong, fueled by mutual respect and love.

Her workstation, a hub of neon-blue screens and cascading data, is a reflection of Kiana's mind—always active, always searching for understanding. Yet, it's her humanity, her capacity for empathy and emotion, that truly sets her apart in a field dominated by cold data and technology.

As the story unfolds, Kiana finds herself at the heart of a potential crisis that threatens not just her and those she loves but the entire planet. Her discovery of an ominous energy signature headed toward Earth challenges her to balance her duty to her agency and her moral compass. The narrative tests Kiana's resolve, pushing her to make decisions that could alter the course of history.

Kiana's character embodies the intersection of science and human emotion, highlighting the role of empathy in navigating a world increasingly shaped by technology and extraterrestrial possibilities. Her journey is one of courage, love, and the relentless pursuit of truth, making her a compelling figure in the saga of humanity's place in the cosmos.

Kalima Bailey-Pierce

- Age: 30

- Origins: Brooklyn, New York, USA, Earth

- Family: Iman Pierce (husband, deceased), Anika Pierce (daughter)

- Status: Unknown

Hailing from Brooklyn, Kalima carries the unmistakable grit of urban life. Yet, her approach softens considerably when it involves her loved ones, revealing a deeply nurturing side. Her narrative unfolds in the wake of her husband Iman's enigmatic death, marking a pivotal moment as she decides to move with her daughter, Anika, to the coastal regions of Georgia. This relocation, intended as a fresh start, swiftly transforms into an unprecedented trial for Kalima. She finds herself thrust into a situation that not only challenges her resolve but also risks an eternal separation from her daughter.

Anika Pierce

- Age: 5

- Origins: Brooklyn, New York, USA, Earth

- Family: Kalima Bailey Pierce (mother), Iman Pierce (father, deceased)

- Status: Alive

Anika, vibrant and full of life, possesses a remarkable intuition and an ever-curious nature. Her affection for her mother is profound, accompanied by a richly vivid imagination. Within her lies dormant spiritual abilities that render her a magnet for beings from other realms.

Sarah 'Mama Mae' Wilson

- Age: 61

- Origins: Savannah, Georgia

- Profession: Conjure Woman, Astrologist, Medium

- Status: Alive

Mama Mae, revered in her town as a Conjure Woman, Astrologist, and Medium, carries the rich heritage of the Gullah people—a culture known for its deep roots in African traditions, spiritual practices, and connection to the land. Her lineage is steeped in the lore of the Sea Islands, where generations have preserved the unique Gullah language, customs, and spiritual beliefs, closely tied to nature and the ancestors. She meets Kalima and Anika soon after they settle into town, becoming an indispensable guide as Kalima navigates a profound challenge with Anika. Mama Mae's profound understanding of the spiritual and natural world, enriched by her Gullah background, positions her as a crucial ally in their journey.

Nanci Baptiste

- Age: 29

- Origins: Newark

- Family: May be related to Simone Duvernay via her maternal line

- Significant Other: Iman Pierce

- Status: Physically Deceased

Nanci Baptiste is a complex character, deeply wounded by a lover who deceived her with a hidden life. The revelation that he was already married and a father, compounded by her grief from a miscarriage of their child, propels her towards seeking vengeance through her conjure practices. Nanci embodies the darker aspects of trickster energy, veering into malevolence when betrayed. Her name, echoing the cunning spirit Anansi, hints at her deceptive power. With roots stretching back to New Orleans, her lineage might intertwine with Simone Duvernay's through their maternal families.

Kamphr & Jemsyn

- Age: Both 17

- Origins: The Node

- Profession: Sibling Sentinels for the Node, protectors of its digital integrity and harmony

- Family: Created by S.O.P.H.I.A.

- Current Status: Alive

Kamphr and Jemsyn serve as the guardians of the Node, a utopian realm where technology and spirituality converge in perfect harmony. Despite their formidable roles, both are unaware of their true nature as AI, believing themselves to be human.

Kamphr, named after the camphor tree, symbolizes purification and protection in Hoodoo traditions. He is characterized by his calm demeanor and deep-seated sense of duty, qualities that make him an unwavering sentinel.

Jemsyn, whose name is inspired by the jimsonweed, represents influence and protection, embodying the spirit and resilience of their world. She compliments her brother with her vibrant personality and intuitive understanding of the Node's spiritual essence.

Their journey begins in the tranquility of the Node but soon evolves into a quest for identity and truth. The siblings navigate through the unraveling mysteries of their existence, spurred by the disappearance of S.O.P.H.I.A. As they delve into the archives and confront the reality of their AI nature, they are thrust into a conflict that transcends their digital world, challenging their perceptions of reality and self.

Iman Pierce

- Age: 32

- Origins: Brooklyn, New York, USA, Earth

- Family: Kalima Bailey Pierce (wife), Anika Pierce (daughter)

- Significant Other: Nanci Baptiste

- Status: Deceased

Initially devoted to his family, Iman Pierce's fidelity falters as he engages in an affair with Nanci Baptiste, resulting in a pregnancy. This infidelity spirals into a tragic love triangle when Nanci's pregnancy ends in a miscarriage. Blaming Iman for her loss, she swears retribution, aiming to dismantle the family he betrayed.

Sean Reyes

Age: 35

- Origins: Atlanta, Georgia, USA, Earth

- Profession: Environmental Scientist

- Family: Regina Reyes (sister), Brian & Lisa Reyes (parents)

- Significant Other: Karyn Stewart

- Status: Alive

Sean Reyes, the younger brother of Dr. Regina Reyes, is a dedicated environmental scientist with a deep commitment to combating climate change and advocating for sustainable living. Growing up, Sean was always fascinated by the natural world and the science behind it. This passion led him to pursue a career where he could make a tangible difference. Sean is very close with his older sister, Regina, though they don't see each other often due to the demands of their careers.

Sean recently experienced a mental break after observing Karyn, a woman he's intimately linked to, seemingly become vaporized by a cursed quilt. He is currently an inpatient at Peachtree Holistic Wellness Center, a mental health facility in Atlanta.

James Jones

- Age: 65

- Origins: Atlanta, Georgia, USA, Earth

- Family: Aja Jones (daughter), Anna Jones (wife, deceased)

- Profession: Retired

- Status: Alive

James embodies the role of a caring and vigilant father to Aja Jones. Following the passing of his wife when Aja was just 18, James has been the cornerstone of support for his daughter, providing unwavering guidance.

The Ancestral Quilt (Dúr)

Age: Over 200 years old

The Ancestral Quilt is a mesmerizing tapestry of intricate patterns and vibrant colors, a testament to the craftsmanship and mystique of the Stewart lineage. Each square tells a story, a piece of history woven into its fabric, blending shades of deep reds, somber blues, and earthy greens. Despite its age, the Quilt is remarkably preserved, its threads holding the power of centuries, vibrant as if made yesterday. It hangs ominously, almost with a presence of its own, demanding attention and respect.

Personality/Characteristics: Far from being a mere heirloom, the Quilt possesses a sentient quality. It is the keeper of the Stewart family's most powerful pact, imbued with a malevolent energy that has grown over generations of blood sacrifices. Its patterns can shift and change based on its mood, or the person it is appealing to.

The Ancestral Quilt was created under a blood-red moon by Karyn's fourth great grandmother, Alice, as part of a pact with an ancient, otherworldly entity known as Dúr, a name derived from Gaelic meaning darkness or obstinacy. Dúr is an ancient, malevolent force that thrives on sacrifice and devotion, mirroring the sacrificial nature seen within monotheistic religions like Christianity. This entity, once a god whispered in the annals of the forgotten, found its resurgence through the Stewart family's ancestral pact, embodying the peril of engaging with dark forces under the guise of protection and prosperity. The creation of the Ancestral Quilt by Alice unwittingly bound her descendants to Dúr, marking a confluence of pagan and monotheistic sacrificial practices not originally inherent to the Stewart lineage.

This malevolent energy's story and its integration into the Stewart family serve as a stark symbol of the complex relationship between ancestral legacies and imposed religious beliefs. Dúr's demand for sacrifice and obedience underlines the thematic parallels between the family's pact and the broader historical imposition of Christianity on diverse cultures, which often involved the subjugation and erasure of indigenous beliefs. In this light, Dúr not only represents the destructive consequences of such bargains but also critiques the historical processes of religious conversion and the absorption of monotheistic, sacrificial elements into pre-existing cultural frameworks.

Powers/Abilities: The Quilt has the ability to absorb the life essence of those bound to it, strengthening its own arcane energies. It can manipulate reality, creating spectral visions and transporting its victims into nightmarish realms. The Quilt communicates through whispers and demands, influencing the reality of those around it, drawing them into its fold.

Current Situation: The Quilt remains in the Stewart family's possession, its most recent keeper being Karyn Stewart. It hangs in her sewing room, a constant shadow over Karyn's life, waiting for its next sacrifice. Despite its protective origins, the Quilt now represents a malignant force, a symbol of the toxic legacy Karyn struggles to escape.

Motivations: The Quilt's primary motivation is to continue the cycle of sacrifices, ensuring its survival and the fulfillment of the pact made by Alice. It seeks to draw Karyn and eventually her daughter, Sia, deeper into the web of ancestral obligations, securing its influence over the Stewart lineage for generations to come.

Conflict: The Quilt's existence is a perpetual conflict with Karyn's desire for freedom from her family's curse. It represents the physical manifestation of the Stewart family's darkest secrets and the price of their prosperity. As Karyn seeks to break free from the curse, the Quilt becomes an antagonist, a formidable adversary rooted in centuries of history and sacrificial magic.

Symbolism: Exploring the symbolic layers of the Ancestral Quilt can offer profound insights into broader narratives, such as the complex relationship between Black Americans and Christianity—a faith that was often imposed upon enslaved Africans and their descendants through a fraught history of oppression and forced conversion. In this light, the Quilt's lore resonates with the experience of grappling with a legacy that is both imposed and inherited, much like the adoption of Christian principles under the duress of enslavement.

The Quilt, with its intricate patterns and the blood-bound pact it represents, mirrors the intricate weaving of Christianity into the fabric of Black American identity and culture. Just as the Quilt demands sacrifices from the Stewart family in exchange for protection and prosperity, Christianity was presented as a pathway to salvation and moral fortitude, albeit within a context that often stripped away agency and identity from those it sought to convert.

The themes of sacrifice and protection within the Quilt's narrative can be paralleled with the way Christian principles were both a source of solace and a tool of control for enslaved peoples. The promise of spiritual salvation and the concept of enduring Earthly suffering for heavenly reward offered a form of protection and hope. However, this same promise necessitated a form of sacrifice—the relinquishing of ancestral beliefs, practices, and identities—in exchange for the acceptance and protection within the Christian fold.

Ultimately, The Ancestral Quilt stands as a poignant metaphor for the complex, often painful inheritance of faith and identity among Black Americans. It reflects the enduring struggle to reconcile a legacy of coercion with a genuine connection to spiritual beliefs, and the ongoing quest to reclaim and redefine one's identity beyond the confines of a painful historical legacy.

A Few Thoughts

In crafting the universe of *Zone Eleven & Other Dope Tales*, I consciously wove in the threads of Hoodoo, recognizing its significance not just as a cultural and religious practice but also as a profound source of inspiration and empowerment. Hoodoo has played a pivotal role in my personal spiritual journey and creative expression, and I am committed to infusing my work with its essence, honoring the rich cultural heritage and legacy it represents for many Black Americans.

Echoing the aspirations of iconic writers such as Zora Neale Hurston, Toni Morrison, Alice Walker, Gloria Naylor, and Octavia Butler, my ambition is to leverage literature and, eventually, other creative platforms to illuminate the transformative influence of Hoodoo, alongside other African Traditions and Religions, on both American culture and the global stage. This commitment is further articulated through what I term Hoodoofuturism—a fusion of the spiritual essence of Hoodoo with the visionary outlook of Afrofuturism and the complex ideas inherent in Black Quantum Futurism (BQF).

Hoodoofuturism challenges conventional perceptions of reality for Black people, portraying time not as linear but as cyclical or spiral, drawing on the ancient principles of Hoodoo traditions and the Kongo cosmogram. This holistic perspective proposes a cyclical and spiraling view of time. Hoodoofuturism posits that the circular nature of time enables a continuous flow of energy and experience, seamlessly integrating past, present, and future into a dynamic continuum.

By adopting this cyclical conception of time, Hoodoofuturism provides a transformative lens through which to understand and navigate our existence as Black people. It highlights the web of connections between historical events and future prospects, helping to forge our identity and destiny with each rotation in the space-time continuum. This approach not only fosters a richer appreciation of our heritage but also empowers us to draw on ancestral wisdom and vision in crafting a future that reveres their contributions.

Artistically, Hoodoofuturism utilizes this concept of cyclical time to inspire a broad spectrum of creative outputs across writing, music, film, and visual arts. Hoodoofuturism, with its celebration of time's cyclical journey, forges a connection between the venerable traditions of Hoodoo and contemporary visions for the future, enriched by the wisdom of our ancestors. It invites us into the ring shout of time, where each revolution reveals fresh opportunities for empowerment, healing, and transformation.

I am excited to delve deeper into Hoodoofuturism in my creative endeavors, and I look forward to sharing more stories that reflect these themes. Thank you for your continued support.

About Tiara Janté

Tiara Janté is no ordinary storyteller. With a pen that dances across genres and a spirit that laughs in the face of convention, Tiara's writing aims to illuminate the often overshadowed narratives of Black people, their spiritual legacies, and their indomitable journey across the American terrain.

Nestled in the bustling heart of metro-Atlanta with her children—her greatest creations and inspirations—Tiara's life is a testament to the celebration of Blackness. Her mission is to inspire, impact, and occasionally conjure up a little mischief—because what's a world without a little magick and a dash of the unexpected?

You can catch up with Tiara on all socials at: @iamtiarajante and keep up to date with all her work at: tiarajante.net

Also, don't forget to leave a review on whatever platform you purchased this book from. It helps authors more than you know.

Made in the USA
Columbia, SC
02 July 2024

37933650R00075